an insiders novel
hold on tight

hold
on tight

an insiders novel

by j. minter

BLOOMSBURY

BLOOMSBURY

Published by Bloomsbury Publishing, New York, London, and Berlin
Distributed to the trade by Holtzbrinck Publishers

Library of Congress Cataloging-in-Publication Data
Minter, J.
Hold on tight : an insiders novel / J. Minter.—1st U.S. ed.
p. cm.
Summary: Five wealthy Manhattan high school juniors visit several colleges while trying to decide which institutions fit their images of who they are and who they want to be.
ISBN-10: 1-58234-719-0 ● ISBN-13: 978-1-58234-719-6
[1. Friendship—Fiction. 2. Self-perception—Fiction. 3. College choice—Fiction. 4. Colleges and universities—Fiction. 5. New York (N.Y.)—Fiction.] I. Title.
PZ7.M67334Hol 2006   [Fic]—dc22   2005031762

Produced by Alloy Entertainment
151 West 26th Street
New York, NY 10001

First U.S. Edition 2006
Typeset by Hewer Text UK Ltd, Edinburgh
Printed in the U.S.A.
10 9 8 7 6 5 4 3 2 1

Bloomsbury Publishing, Children's Books, U.S.A.
175 Fifth Avenue, New York, NY 10010

All papers used by Bloomsbury Publishing are natural, recyclable products made from wood grown in well-managed forests. The manufacturing processes conform to the environmental regulations of the country of origin.

for EER

what i could really use is a little time away from it all . . .

When I stepped out of my apartment Friday morning with the vague idea of getting a cup of coffee and a chocolate croissant and heading up to school, I had no idea I wouldn't be coming back until Sunday night.

My John Fluevog croc loafers hit the pavement and I was suddenly overcome with that feeling all Manhattanites experience when they've forgotten to leave our hallowed island for far too long. The streets were full of people carrying bulky bags and moving way too slow, and the May air felt dense and sooty. It's like the population of the city doubles when it's warm like this, I swear, and that kind of overcrowding can really trigger the ol' fight or flight mechanism. (In my case, that would mostly be flight.) Now that my friends and I are at the end of our junior year, all anybody can talk about is which colleges they're applying to and what percentage of applicants Harvard accepts a year and blah blah blah—that *alone* could make a guy want to catch a cab to Grand Central and hop the next train out of here.

The second sign that I wasn't going to be sleeping in my own bed that night was the phone call I received just as I was on my way out the door. It was my brother Ted, who's a sophomore up at Vassar—he just wanted to let me know that he'd heard about all the bad stuff that went down with our stepbrother Rob a month ago. (Or ex-stepbrother, as I prefer to think of him, if you can divorce a step-sibling without your dad divorcing his absurdly wealthy British-Venezuelan wife.) Rob *did* try to ruin my life, but realistically, so did I. See, *New York* magazine crowns one guy Hottest Private School Boy every spring, and I wanted that guy to be me. A little too much. So when it was my friend Arno who was picked, I spent an interminably long week acting like a total jackass, alienating my friends, and really messing up with my girl, too.

Anyway, it all worked out—the crew is back together, and it's probably a good thing that Flan and I broke up—but it was still nice to hear from Ted. The thing is, I feel kind of burnt on the whole

New York party scene right now, and my older brother Ted is this intensely grounded, earnest guy. I know I haven't said much about him before, but, well, we're awfully . . . different. He's my brother, so I wouldn't want to say he isn't *cool*, but suffice it to say that, he hasn't spent a whole lot of time dreaming about what it would mean to be Hottest Private School Boy. And there *certainly* was never any risk of him being chosen. So when I told him I had to go, he said, "It was really good to reconnect with you, Jonathan. You should come up and see me at school sometime." Normally if someone said that, I'd laugh, because the chance of them talking that way and not being sarcastic is about as good as finding your true love in the backroom at Marquee at two a.m., but with my brother it's different. He's sincere. To a fault. A totally dorky, but lovable fault.

Then, as I was walking up Fifth, I thought, yeah, I *should* go see him.

The third unheeded sign was the simple fact that my friends—David, Mickey, Patch and Arno—are the guys they are. And crazy shit just tends to happen. That's definitely something I should know by now. After all, Mickey Pardo recently convinced a bunch of kids we know—all of them pretty

sophisticated, but still, you know, in high school—
to pose for him. In a restaurant. As a group. Naked.
But wait—you're going to hear a whole lot more
about that in a minute.

As I rounded the corner onto West Twelfth
Street and looked for a cab, my phone started
buzzing in my pocket.

"This is Jonathan," I said, very calmly flipping
my phone open.

"J, it's Mickey," Mickey said, and his voice didn't
sound calm in the least. "I need your help."

"What's up?" I tried to redirect all my attention
from the Fluevogs—it had just occurred to me that
they might be a tad garish—to what had Mickey so
rattled. (Mickey is not a guy easily rattled, I might
add, although high-octane crises do tend to follow
him around. His father is this famous sculptor,
Ricardo Pardo, and his mom is an ex-model and
actually super-hot for a mom. It's basically a high-
octane household.)

"Remember how I'm supposed to lecture this
weekend?"

"Um, lecture?"

"Yeah, you know, on the photo project . . ."

Yes, that would be the naked restaurant photo
project. I paused a moment, and tried to re-wrap

my mind around the kind of world we live in. "Where are you lecturing, the basement of Pastis?" I asked.

"Naw, man, it's at some college."

"You were asked to lecture at a *college?*"

"Why is that surprising?" In the background, it sounded like Mickey had knocked over a mighty stack of something. "Yeah, I think the art department asked me. Listen, it's tomorrow night at like seven or something, but I'm supposed to be up there tonight because they reserved a place for me at this cottage and they're paying me a stipend and—"

"A *stipend?*" Like I said, I should have learned to expect this kind of thing by now. But in the moment, I was just trying to take it all in and make sense of it.

"Yeah, whatever, like a thousand dollars. Anyway, how am I going to get there? J, you know how to uh—plan travel. It's got to be tonight."

"What college is putting you up and paying you money for a talk about your naked photos?"

"Vassar? *The Vassar Art Department has cordially invited you . . .*" Mickey started reading something into the phone. "So, how do we get there?"

The very same Vassar my brother Ted goes to. It was a sign. I told Mickey that I was coming over, and slipped my phone into one of the back pockets of my Yanuk six-pocket jeans. Then I turned and started walking in the other direction, back downtown, to the huge converted warehouse where the Pardos live.

what *wouldn't* mickey pardo do
for a thousand dollars?

"Gah!" Mickey screamed from under his down comforter.

The massive house where the Pardo family lived and worked was full of noise, although Mickey's room was perhaps the noisiest. He had recently taken over a spare bedroom that his father's art assistants occasionally slept in when the workday went late. The floor was paint-splattered concrete, and the bed was a loft made out of chrome and driftwood. He had switched rooms mostly because the old room reminded him of his longtime girlfriend, Philippa Frady, who had recently come out as a lesbian and broken up with him.

The new room already was full of his stuff, particularly the loft part, where he was now searching for the directions the Vassar people had sent him. He thought they were around here on the bed somewhere, but with all the CDs, rumpled T-shirts, and cans of spray paint scattered around, he couldn't help but wonder where he'd actually been sleeping. Certainly not here. The big Ricardo Pardo–made couch in the living room? Whatever—he didn't have time to think about it right now.

He turned up the live, bootlegged Babyshambles recording that was blasting through the five speakers he'd hooked up in various corners of the new room. Mickey, who was attractive in a rough, simian way—no one would call him handsome, but lots of girls thought he was hot anyway—air guitared briefly. Then he went back to tearing through the piles of papers he'd practiced tagging on and schoolbooks that had somehow arrived in his room. Finally he found the piece of paper he had been looking for. It was on Vassar letterhead and it included various instructions on how to get to the school, what time his lecture was scheduled for, how long he should speak, and so on. It also reminded him that, on completion of his lecture duties, he would be offered a thousand dollar stipend.

"Score," he muttered to himself.

Since Mickey had successfully staged a nude restaurant photo shoot, he'd been getting a lot of attention. Most of the photos had ended up on Web sites, and there had been some newspaper and magazine attention. He'd been invited to several gallery openings, and been asked to sit on a panel or two, and some public radio person had wanted to interview him. But his father was a famous artist, and

Mickey's best friend, Arno Wildenburger, was the son of famous art dealers, so none of this felt all that special to him. He'd been declining the offers, mostly. But because his parents kept cutting off his cash flow for some behavioral reason or other, when these Vassar people had thrown money in the mix, he had called them right away and said he'd be there and could they make the check out to cash?

Now he just had to find a way out of the city, get his overgrown thicket of dark hair in order, and think of something to say at this lecture-thingy that wouldn't get that thousand dollar offer taken away. Luckily, his dad's studio manager, Caselli, liked Mickey in spite of his many antics, and had converted the film from the photo shoot into slides. Mickey was sure that those were around here somewhere, too.

It wasn't that Mickey didn't care about giving a good lecture—he did. He'd never been into school much, and the idea that maybe he could be an artist like his dad was novel and cool. So he did want to say funny, smart things at the lecture tomorrow. He had just never really seen the point in preparing for stuff.

Mickey tucked the letter into the pocket of his cut-off seersucker suit pants, and half-climbed, half-dove down the loft's ladder. When he hit the floor he was happy to find himself face to face with his friend Jonathan.

"Hey man!" Jonathan shouted over the music. He was

wearing some very loud shoes and a suede bomber jacket that the weather definitely didn't call for. For once, Mickey was kind of psyched on something Jonathan was wearing.

"Thanks for coming over!" Mickey shouted back. He gave Jonathan his usual, tackle-style hug; Mickey was not a tall guy, and his grip was powerful. "And for the unstated offer to save my sorry ass."

"So," Jonathan said, locating the universal remote and turning down the music. "What's the deal? What time are you supposed to be there?"

"Well, it says in this letter . . ." Mickey handed over the typed offer on Vassar letterhead for Jonathan's perusal.

Jonathan skimmed it and then said, "Okay, looks like you're supposed to meet the chair of the Art Department at five. It's almost eleven now, and it takes about two hours to get to Vassar. You're with me?"

"Yup. Sounds like we've got lots o' time."

"Right, but that's two hours by car, and last I checked neither one of us has a license," Jonathan said, as though he were administering a quiz. "Now, who do we know who has a license?"

Mickey looked at him blankly. "What are you talking about? *I* drive all the time."

"Yeah, I know. But don't you think, given your new stature, it would be nice to arrive *without* police intervention?"

"You're probably right," Mickey said, because Jonathan usually was.

"Good. Have you seen Patch—'cause I know he has a license."

"Great! Let's go find Patch." Mickey slapped his hands together. "Oh, the slides. I need the slides." He started kicking through the piles of stuff he had left all over his bedroom floor. "Shit, I knew I should have paid more attention to those."

"These slides?" Jonathan asked, lifting a slide carousel off the ground.

Mickey was about to give Jonathan another tackle hug, but then reconsidered. "Let's go."

Jonathan followed Mickey down the hall, which was twenty feet high and had an eerie, cathedral-like feel. The walls were decorated with early Pardo wall sculptures made out of half-demolished farm equipment. On their way out they passed the studio, where Ricardo's latest project was being constructed by a small army of tattooed assistants amid a blaze of sparks.

"Do you think I need to do something about my hair?" Mickey said as he swung the industrial metal door closed and reset the alarm.

Jonathan shrugged. "They saw the pictures. They can't say they didn't know what they were getting."

"Sometimes teenagers can be very callous," Dr. Guy Beller said, stroking his graying beard and looking at Arno Wildenburger as though he had just made the profoundest of observations.

No shit, Arno thought, although he just nodded and pushed back into the couch in Dr. Beller's spare Tribeca office.

Everyone agreed that Arno, who was half-Brazilian, half-German and six feet tall, was handsome. But he liked to think—with his defined features and dark hair—that he was never quite so good-looking as when he brooded.

Of course, thus far, his brooding had only landed him in therapy.

This moping and soul-searching was new for Arno, and had been brought about mostly by a series of unusual rejections. One moment he was being named the Hottest Private School Boy in Manhattan by *New York* magazine, and being pursued by not one but three lank, bleach-blond Upper East Side party girls; the next it was publicly revealed that he was actually the magazine's *second* choice, and those party girls had changed their cell phone numbers just to further humiliate and avoid him. The whole experience had had a really negative effect on his sense of self.

That was how he had ended up having twice-weekly sessions with Dr. Beller, a colleague of Arno's friend David's dad.

Dr. Beller gave Arno a nod. "Do you agree?"

"Oh yeah. I know this sounds weird, but it seems like girls can be even more cruel than guys sometimes," Arno said. "It was pretty traumatic for me, being treated like, you know, just any other pretty face."

Dr. Beller leaned his elbows on his knees and gave Arno a searching look. After a pause, he said, "Would you say things come easy to you?"

"Um, well, usually," Arno said warily, "I guess."

"Would you say that—because of the way you look, the way you dress—people 'hand you' things?" Dr. Beller asked, making quotation marks with his long, slender fingers. Dr. Beller was even taller than Arno and he took up an awful lot of space in the room. He kept coming forward and crouching and staring, too, which wasn't making Arno more relaxed.

"Um, maybe," Arno said darkly. "But it sure doesn't feel that way lately."

"How did it feel to be the Hottest Private School Boy?" Dr. Beller went on, again using his too-long fingers to make lots of quotes.

For a moment, Arno couldn't help himself—his wide mouth broke into a smile, and the gorgeous creases in his cheeks emerged. "It's was awesome, just getting attention, everyone wants to know you, getting into all the hottest clubs. Not that I couldn't get in before, but everything was amplified, you know?"

Dr. Beller nodded thoughtfully. "Have you ever gone out with a woman who wasn't beautiful?" he asked.

Arno chuckled. "Nope, they're always hot chicks."

Dr. Beller sighed, and leaned back in his chair. "What I'm trying to get at is that *maybe* it isn't entirely the world's fault that *you're* not feeling so hot. Maybe the fault is fifty percent the world's, fifty percent yours."

Arno stared out the window at the skyline of expensive penthouses converted from industrial buildings and wondered how *that* could be.

"These young women you were hanging out with, for instance. They treated you poorly, no doubt about that. But I'm not sure what you were doing with these 'ladies,'" Dr. Beller again made the quotation marks, "in the first place."

Arno shrugged. "It was just a good time . . ."

"Perhaps what you need, in your life right now, is more than a good time." Dr. Beller stood up so that he was looking down on his patient. "Rather than fun—a very overrated pursuit, in my opinion—and rather than 'hot chicks,' perhaps you should be seeking a meaningful relationship."

Arno noticed for the first time how well-dressed Dr. Beller was, and how totally tall, and that made Arno respect him just a little bit more. "Meaningful relationship?" he repeated.

"Arno, what I'm trying to say is, I think you need some depth."

"Depth?" Arno said. He was still trying to get a handle on the word when his cell went off in his pocket. "Wildenburger," he said, flipping open his new phone. It was silver and tiny, and just as he had expected, it made him feel very cool and tech-savvy.

"Hey, man. It's Jonathan. Listen, have you seen Patch?"

"No. Where are you?" Arno asked, signaling to Dr. Beller that he would just be a moment. Dr. Beller gestured to him that it was all right.

"Mickey's house."

Arno stood up and turned away from Dr. Beller, as though that might prevent him from hearing Arno's conversation. "I'll come over," he said. "What's brewing?"

"Mickey, believe this or not, was asked to lecture at Vassar."

"On what? The hazards of substance abuse?"

"Maybe you forgot your friend is a big artist now? Anyway, you haven't heard from Patch? We need someone to drive us up there, and Patch is the only driver we know."

"Can I come?"

"To Vassar? Why do you want to come to Vassar? You know you wilt like a daisy when you're taken outside urban areas."

"Yeah, I know," Arno said, glancing toward Dr. Beller. "But I've been thinking about getting a new girl, and that maybe it should be a . . . you know . . . *meaningful* relationship. That's what college girls are into, right?" In Arno's mind, he pictured an ivory skinned creature lounging on a settee with a book by one of those French guys, Camus or whoever. They could read it aloud to each other and hold hands and he could stare deep into her eyes. That sounded pretty meaningful.

"I guess," Jonathan said doubtfully. "Anyway, you want in? Then get over here and help us find Patch."

Arno hung up the phone, and turned back to his therapist. "Look Doc, I gotta run."

"That's too bad," Dr. Beller said evenly. "I thought we were really getting somewhere."

"But I'll see you next week, right?" Arno said. He actually wanted to, too.

"Of course. But Arno? Try and think about what we've discussed for next week. *Depth*, Arno. Think about depth."

Arno promised he would think about depth, and then he headed for Mickey's house.

David Grobart was lounging in his bedroom in the West Village, making weekend plans with a girl he couldn't quite remember meeting but who definitely remembered him. She even knew about the long scar that ran from his hipbone to his lower rib, a souvenir from that time in sixth grade when he'd tried to be a skateboarder. David had always been the guy in his group who was the least smooth with girls, but ever since he'd been prominently featured in his friend Mickey's nude photo shoot, his relative lack of smoothness had become pretty much irrelevant.

He'd been told there were whole websites dedicated to his abs.

David was the best basketball player at Potterton, and he had long, powerful, basketball-player arms. He stretched them over his head in a big, yawny gesture and listened to this girl Mia, who knew all about his scar, tell him what she was going to wear to the party at Lisa Brenner's that weekend.

"So, you're coming with me?" she asked breathlessly. He had no idea who this girl was, but he loved the sound of her voice.

"Yeah, I don't *think* I have anything to do that night," David said. "Oh wait, can you hold on a sec? I have someone on the other line."

"Okay, but don't leave me sitting here forever," she said, in a way that was jokily chastising and kind of made him think that was *exactly* what he should do, just to find out what the consequences were.

David hit the flash button. "What's up?"

"David? It's Jonathan. Have you seen Patch?"

"Um, no," David said. It was a weird question, because if Jonathan hadn't seen Patch, it probably meant that David hadn't seen him, either.

"Damn, all right," Jonathan said disappointedly. "You don't have basketball practice tonight, do you?"

"Nope, season's over."

"Good. Because we're going to Vassar."

"Tonight?"

"Yeah. Mickey's going to lecture to the Art Department, and Patch has to go because he's the only one who can drive, and Arno wants to go meet some un-shallow girls, and I'm going to try and hang out with Ted. Obviously, you should come, too."

"I think I have a date," David said. That thought,

which had made him so happy a minute ago, made him feel sort of sad when he said it now.

"You *think* you have a date? With who?"

"Um, this girl Mia. She says we met her at the Hudson Hotel bar a couple of weeks ago?"

"Oh. Huh. Do you remember who she is?"

"No."

"Well, I think you should postpone the big date with the girl you can't remember and come to Vassar with us. There will be girls you don't remember there, too."

David thought about this for a moment, and was about to say that canceling the date like that didn't really seem like a very nice way to treat a girl, when his mom, Hilary Grobart, came barging through the door. His mother, like his father, was a therapist, and she talked a lot about how she protected and valued and believed in David's privacy. Apparently, this was in contrast to a lot of her patients. It was also more in theory than in practice.

"David, have you seen the phone?" she asked.

"Yeah, I'm talking to Jonathan on it," he said, and then added, unnecessarily, "He's going up to Vassar this weekend."

"I didn't know Jonathan was considering Vassar," his mother paused, twisting at her Live Strong bracelet. "Maybe you should go, as well?"

"Can I?"

"Don't you think that's a good idea?"

All the attention from mysterious girls with soft, girly voices, like Mia, was new, and David felt nervous giving that up for even a couple days, as though it might all evaporate. But he also hated being left behind by his friends. That was something he had already experienced plenty.

"Jonathan, I gotta go. I'll meet you at Patch's?"

"Great," Jonathan said. "I'll see you soon, man."

As soon as David hung up the phone, his mother took it out of his hand and began dialing. She walked out of his room, and as she headed down the hall, he could hear her saying, "Who? Mia? Could you maybe be trying to reach a different David Grobart?"

David decided that if he were Arno, he wouldn't feel bad about ditching this Mia girl, and that got him as far as stuffing a change of clothes, his iPod, and some English homework into his backpack. Then he pulled his oversized Potterton hoodie over his head and walked into the living room.

"Right, right. Thanks. Bye-bye," his mother was saying. She was sitting on the black leather couch in the living room, underneath the collection of African masks that she and David's father had acquired while on their midlife crisis stint in the Peace Corps. She hung up the phone and looked at David. "Well, you can't go in that."

"Go where? In what?"

"To your interview. In a hoodie."

"Um, interview?"

"Yes, sweetie. We're extremely lucky because they usually don't give interviews on the weekends, but I guess spring is a very busy time of year for prospective student visitors. Frightening, I know. But they do, occasionally, hold weekend interviews, and now you've got one. I just called. So I really don't think you should wear a sweatshirt. It would send the wrong signal, don't you think?"

"Uh, this was more of an informal, checking-out-the-school kind of thing," David said. He sounded unconvincing even to himself.

"David, this is a very competitive time of year. If you're not going to make this trip a meaningful one, you should stay in the city. After all, there's the SAT to study for, you should keep in shape for basketball, there's volunteering, your schoolwork, and . . . well, just so many things." His mom looked kind of exhausted just thinking about it. David, as usual, didn't have the heart to fight her when she was down.

"Okay, Mom. When's the interview?"

"Eleven-thirty, tomorrow morning. Here's the information," she said, handing him one of her business cards, which had the name and office location of his interviewer scrawled on the back. On the front side it said Hilary Grobart, Ph.D., Clinical Psychologist, Intuitive. Lately his mother, who had made her name with a line of self-help books, was expanding her practice to include more "experimental" treatments. David took the card and watched as his mother stood up and walked to the closet in the hall where they kept all their winter coats. "Now, where's your suit?"

"Mom, that's the suit I wore to Great Aunt Edie's funeral. Two years ago." David winced at the black wool suit his mother had pulled from the closet. It had been too small when she bought it for him, and he feared what it would look like on him now. "Don't you think it'll fit sort of funny?"

"David, I really think you're making a problem where there isn't one," his mother said. "But put it on, let's see."

David tried to make a face that would make his mother understand that she was treating him like a child, but the phone rang so she didn't notice. She answered, and then handed the phone to her son. "It's for you," she said.

"Hello?" he said into the receiver.

"David, why haven't you left yet?" Jonathan asked.

"I'm coming, I'm coming!" David said.

"Well, hurry up, okay?"

"Okay," he said, and hung up. David turned to his mother; she was giving him a stern look, so he went resignedly into the hall bathroom and put on the suit. It was worse than he could have imagined. The pants were a good five inches above his ankles, and his wrists were entirely exposed. He stepped back into the hall. "Mom," he whined, sounding a little bit like a five-year-old, "I look like a clown."

"I think you look handsome," she said. "And you *have* to wear a suit. Otherwise, what will they think? They'll think you were raised by wolves!"

The phone rang again. David picked it up. "What's up . . . ," he said.

"Why haven't you left yet?" Jonathan asked.

"I'm coming, I'm coming." David shot back nervously. He hung up and looked at his mother. There was nothing about her that suggested she was going to budge. David weighed the embarrassment of going out looking like his mommy had dressed him in his junior high graduation suit versus the misery of being left behind.

"Thanks again, Mom," he said. "I'll see you Monday!"

"But David, you can't *wear* your suit now!" His

mother called after him, as he hurried for the door and the safety of his nice, sane friends.

Of course, it wasn't until he saw Jonathan standing outside the Floods' house that David realized he'd left his duffel—and all his normal clothes—behind.

it's a brave girl who tries to domesticate patch

"But the thing is, you look adorable in surf shorts. And how often are you going to be wearing surf shorts at Yale or Swarthmore or some other stuffy East Coast school?"

Patch Flood, who was tall and lanky, had been called adorable before, but hearing it never got any easier. He twisted uncomfortably on the soft, light-gray leather seats of his parents' yellow Mercedes, stretching his legs out so that his ankles rested against the open window frame. Then he pulled his faded Yankees hat down over his overgrown sandy hair as though that might convey to his girlfriend, Greta O'Grady, who was currently sitting on her deck in Santa Cruz, California, looking at an ocean that was not the Atlantic, how weird that word made him feel.

He had taken to making calls from the car, because he lived with two sisters who were very into eavesdropping.

Patch had met Greta on an educational cruise over the winter, and he was now having a bicoastal, cell-phone enabled relationship with her. It certainly wasn't convenient, but then, he'd never met a girl remotely as cool as Greta. She was so cool that he was willing to have the millionth argument with her about whether they should go to college together on her coast or his.

"I think you might be forgetting that college only takes up like eight months of the year," he said. "I mean, don't you think we should spend our collegiate years in a classroom instead of at the beach?"

"Patch Flood, attendance king of the eastern seaboard," Greta hooted. "You can't tell me you're going to stop playing hooky now. Besides, hello, redwoods? I mean, you've been to California. I can't believe I have to convince you how nice it would be for us to live here. Together."

"Hey, I know California is gorgeous. But realistically, you're about as much gorgeous as I can handle." Patch rarely resorted to lines of this kind, but when he did, they were frighteningly effective. Except, perhaps, on Greta, who was a little bit shy and a little bit wild and didn't seem remotely interested in being romanced in any of the usual ways.

"Flattery is not going to make me want to go live in an overcrowded, bricked-in city that's freezing four months out of the year. Four months of the *academic* year."

"Maybe you'd end up liking it. You know, learning about the seasons, watching fall turn to winter. That's when snow falls from the sky. Then you can roll around in it. It's very academic."

There was a long silence, and then Patch could hear Greta standing up and walking somewhere. He could tell from the sound that she was wearing flip-flops. Greta had a body that was strong and freckled from crew practice, but she had small, perfectly pale feet with toenails like little red jewels. Patch was thinking about them distractedly, when she cut in with a hushed "Look, Patch, do you want to go to the same school as me and live together and be crazy and fun and in love or not? I mean, it seems to me like you can't let go *at all*. I mean, really, seriously, what is so great about New York? What are you so afraid of leaving behind?"

At the abrupt change in tone, Patch pulled his legs in and jerked himself upright. That was when he saw three sets of eyes peering down on him—Mickey, Arno and Jonathan. Patch immediately fumbled his cell phone.

"Patch," Jonathan said, leaning in against the window frame, "you've been wearing that hat since 1999. Don't you think it's time to get a new one?"

"Hi guys," Patch said as he tried to locate his phone. "Can you give me a couple?"

"A couple what?" Mickey said. "Cuz I think you're already in one."

"Mickey, shut up," Jonathan scolded.

"A couple minutes," Patch said. "Can you give me a couple minutes?"

"Patch?" he heard Greta say, as he grabbed the phone from the floor. He reached for the window crank, and then he remembered that the windows were automated.

"Yeah, I'm still here. My friends just showed up. Look, all I want to do is go to the same school as you. I just never considered going West Coast. And that's weird for me."

"I know," Greta said. "I'm sorry. I know this is a decision we really have to make together and . . ."

"Um, excuse me, Patch?" Jonathan was sort of leaning in through the window now, and he had a very urgent look on his face.

"Greta, can you hold on?" Patch asked. "What's up, J?"

"We have to go to Vassar. Now. Can you drive us?"

Patch considered this for a moment, and then he said into his phone: "Hey apple blossom, if I check out Vassar for us this weekend, will you check out Stanford?"

"You mean, you'll consider going to Stanford?"

"Yes," Patch answered.

"If we *do* go to Vassar, can we get a puppy?"

"Two," Patch said.

"Okay, yes then."

"Great. I've got to go now."

"Yeah, me too. I miss you."

"I miss you too," Patch said, noticing as he did that Jonathan was rolling his eyes.

"Call me tonight?" Greta asked.

"Okay." Patch hung up and tossed the phone onto the front passenger seat. He looked at his three friends, who were all trying in a sort of half-assed way not to giggle. Patch climbed into the front seat and put the key in the ignition.

"You all can laugh if you want to," he said. "But I'm still the only one who can drive you weirdos to Vassar."

Jonathan opened the back door and scooted into the middle seat with Mickey behind him. Arno walked around and took shotgun. Patch was about to pull out when he saw a tall guy walking toward them in the middle of the street. He was wearing a suit that made him look like the stranger in a black and white movie.

"Who's the bible salesman?" Jonathan said from the backseat.

"Who died?" Mickey shouted out the window.

David came trotting up to the car and bent over to peer in. "You guys weren't going to leave without me were you? Because I left all my clothes at my house and—"

"Dude," Anro interrupted. "That suit is not going to make girls think you are hot."

"Except in the literal sense, of course," Jonathan said. "Why are you wearing a dark-colored, wool-blend suit on one of the warmest days of the spring? Also, is that a mod outfit? Because unless you're trying out for a part in *Austin Powers 4*, I think that suit is a shade too small for you."

"Ha, ha," David deadpanned. "Now, can we just swing by my house and grab my stuff?"

"Not a chance," Mickey said as he opened the canary yellow Mercedes door. "We've got places to be . . ."

my guys and I move slowly, slowly northward

"No way, you do *not* have to talk to your girl again . . . ," Mickey yelled. I was sitting in the middle of a back seat that was luxury, but not exactly luxurious, so I really heard that one. Arno, up in the front, added loudly: "Can't you see our boy is whipped?"

"I'll call you back in a second . . . ," Patch said before hanging up and putting his phone back on the dashboard. Then he made a sudden turn and brought us into our third rest area of the afternoon.

Secretly I was happy that we had stopped again, what with me somehow having been assigned the middle seat and all, although teasing Patch felt like the natural thing to do. Patch is kind of day-dreamy and the most elusive of my friends, which of course makes girls crush on him even more than they would in the first place. So now that he actually, no joke, cares about just one girl, it's hard not to want to talk a little bit of good-natured shit.

And his girlfriend, Greta, lives in California, so that only makes it more funny—Patch has never been one to abuse his cell phone minutes, you see, and now that's all he seems to be doing.

"Did you just want to check with her if it's okay to go over sixty-five?" I asked. Patch shot me an *Et tu, Brute?* look in the rearview mirror, pulled up the emergency break, and got out of the car. Then we all tumbled out, too.

The first time we'd stopped, at the very first gas station on the other side of the George Washington Bridge, nobody had said anything. We were out of the city, and that simple fact had tranquilized us all somewhat. Apparently Patch and Greta had had some sort of fight (although I couldn't figure out who was apologizing to who), and Patch talked on the cell phone for a good half hour while the rest of us got big Cokes and watched the traffic go by.

The second time, it was actually Mickey's fault because he'd forgotten to piss before we got back in the car at the gas station, and only after we'd all gotten out to stretch our legs did Patch's phone ring. Apparently, that time Greta was just calling back with her initial impressions of Stanford, where she'd just arrived.

Now we were standing around our third road-side convenience store, with a lot of greenery surrounding us and some birds chirping. Patch walked away, talking on his cell phone, and stopped just as soon as he knew we couldn't hear him anymore.

"This is too weird," David said. Arno and Mickey and I had sat down on a log, but David was standing up in this kind of rigid position. He'd tried on the clothes we'd all packed at the last rest stop, but all our worn T-shirts had fit his lank basketball-player frame like belly shirts, and now he was back in his black suit. Poor guy.

"What?" Arno said. "You mean how Patch has gotten all Mr. Greta on us?" He looked wistfully over at Patch, who was talking and tugging on his Yankees cap like he was trying to psych out a batter. "It's going to bite us all, sooner or later," he added cryptically.

"Hey man, are you getting hot or what?" I asked.

David blinked at me in the bright sunlight. I instantly wished I hadn't brought the suit thing up.

"Do I look really stupid?" he asked.

"Nah, just a little stupid," Mickey said. "Or just a little bit little."

"Not even," I said. "It's sort of cool, actually. I

was thinking of adding a little mod to my look, too, but it looks like you beat me to it."

David finally smiled, which was a relief. Sometimes you just have to lie—just a little bit—with your friends, you know what I mean? Although, to give him credit, David has this new confidence that is really working for him. He's always been the guy with the nice face and the wrong hair—you see this all the time—but lately he's been wearing his hair in a very trimmed, Luke Wilson style that really works for him. Even when he's wearing a kid's suit.

"I'm going to go see if they have any of those red pistachios," Mickey said, standing up and making a lip-smacking sound. "You guys want anything?"

I shook my head and David sat down on the log in the space that Mickey had vacated.

"Maybe I shouldn't have come," he said.

"What do you mean?" I said. "Of course you should have come. What were you going to do in Manhattan with all of us gone, anyway?"

"Yeah, that's true. I just haven't really dated anyone since Amanda, and that Mia girl sounded kind of hot."

"*Sounded* hot?" I said. This was vintage David. "You don't even know what she looks like, and you're already moping about her."

"I am not," David said, a little defensively.

"Look, I just don't want to see you get into another thing like what you had with Amanda, which was such an Exhibit A see-saw relationship. The reason she could bring you so low was the same reason she could bring so high. You were way too impressed by her. You've got to be careful on that see-saw, man."

There was a long uncomfortable silence, which I hoped indicated that David was taking in what I'd said, and then he changed the subject.

"You excited to see Ted?" he asked.

"Yeah," I said. And actually, I really was. I'd been so focused on getting my guys together for the last few hours that I'd almost forgotten about Ted and the fact that I was going to see him. Ted isn't flashy or anything, and people forget about him a lot, but that's too bad, because he's a super-good guy.

"Oh yeah, I forgot Ted went to Vassar," Arno said. "Is he still writing letters to congress about a woman's right to choose and shit?"

"Hey, man, I know Ted doesn't spend his nights like we do, and he listens to music from like 1995, but he's my brother and he, um . . . he cares about stuff," I said. The truth was, I hadn't seen Ted all that much since he started college almost two years ago. He'd spent last summer doing Habitat for Humanity down near New Orleans, and there'd always been a party or something on the weekends he came home.

"I didn't mean that in a bad way," Arno said.

"I know."

"Your brother's really cool," Arno continued. This was when I realized that he must be feeling kind of wounded about something, because usually he wouldn't even notice that he'd said something retarded.

"Ted has always been really nice to me," David said. Then, as though he could hear that reverberating uncooly in his brain, he added, "But isn't he always nice to everyone? I could totally see him lecturing us on how to better understand the plight of pigeons, what with all the social injustices they've endured."

"Remember how he always used to tell us not to call each other 'retarded' when we did stupid things, because it was insulting to handicapped people?" Arno said.

"Yeah," I said. "He used to get all flustered and red, like *really* mad about it. He'd still be taking about it at home."

"That was so retarded," Arno said.

We all laughed at that, but I got psyched all over again to see Ted. After all, being cool around him was pretty effortless.

"What do you think they're talking about?" Arno said, abruptly changing the subject. We all looked. "I mean, I find this as freaking bizarre as the rest of you, but they must have something major between them to be going on like this, you know what I mean?"

Patch looked over at us, and saw that we were all staring. For some reason, none of us looked away. He said something into the phone, and then he put it back in his pocket and started walking toward us. He was shaking his head, and kind of chuckling.

"You guys look like you're ready to hit the road," he said as he approached.

We all stood, and as we did we heard a skidding of gravel just behind us. I turned, slowly it seemed, and that's when I saw Mickey, a ripped open bag of red pistachios hanging from his teeth and his bright red palms out in front of him, barreling in our direction.

he's not my little ted anymore

"I still think that's going to come off," Mickey said for maybe the hundredth time. The light was fading from the sky as Patch steered the car slowly through the Vassar campus. David, who had two large, red handprints on his clean, white dress shirt, looked pained that the topic had come up again. "Come on, man," Mickey continued, "I'll buy you another shirt. A Vassar one. Your interviewer will flip for that."

"It's cool," David said, although he didn't look like he meant it. He kept looking straight ahead, at all the big leafy trees and quaint brick buildings.

"Or maybe," Mickey continued, his eyes getting kind of glassy, "I could sign it, the way Picasso would sign his napkin doodles to pay for dinner . . ."

I was relieved that at just that moment I saw Ted, standing at the edge of the quad with his hands stuffed into knee-length, cutoff jeans, and instead of saying, "Mickey, you are *not* Picasso," I got to say, "There he is, pull over."

Patch pulled the Mercedes up onto the lawn, and then I got out and waved at my brother. Ted looks a lot like me, except a little bit taller and a lot sloppier: his dark blond hair was overgrown and flopping in his eyes, and he was wearing the kind of stretched and faded T-shirt that girls love to borrow to sleep in. As he hugged me and slapped me on the back, I couldn't help but notice the jean cutoffs again. They were stylish, like something you would see on aviator-sporting dudes in Williamsburg. Was Ted rocking a hipster trend, or had he just cluelessly cropped some old pants? Clearly I was going to have to investigate further.

"Hey Bro," he said, throwing his arms around me. "It sure is good to see you."

Then he turned to my guys and started saying his hellos. "Nice suit," he said to David. Then he added, without a hint of sarcasm, "Is that artistically embellished?"

David finally cracked a smile at that one, and then he and Ted gave each other back-patting hugs. "Nope, though this one might have you believe otherwise." He jerked his head in Mickey's direction.

"Mi*hick*ster," Ted said, high-fiving Mickey. "I've heard some very positive buzz about your event tomorrow night, Bro. Looking forward, looking forward. Arno, Patch, good to see you. I think there's some fun stuff going on tonight, so let's go get you guys settled, and then we can hit the town, as it were."

"Hit the town" is a phrase I find incomparably dorky, but it wasn't surprising coming out of Ted's mouth. Back when Ted was in high school, he was always saying totally cringe-worthy things.

We followed Ted toward a big brick building with a peaked roof and lots of gothic-looking windows. There were kids on the grass out front, tossing Frisbees and reading and chatting. There were a few couples very publicly making out, too, which made me forget where I was for a minute and yearn for Flan.

"Wow, this really looks like college," I said, remembering again why we'd come, and thinking it would be sort of cool to take a four-year time-out from the city and live in the country and read books about British history or the lives of insects or whatever.

"Yeah, no kidding," Ted said.

As we walked across the field—the smell of

grass almost overwhelming—people kept looking up at Ted and smiling, or waving at him and calling out his name. When I was a freshman at Gissing and Ted was a senior, I always got the feeling that nobody knew who he was and now it felt like people perked right up when they saw him.

When we got to the big oak door of the building, he swiped his ID card and led us into a dark hallway.

"Does it smell funny in here?" I asked, because it kind of did. Like old broccoli or something.

Ted laughed gently and looked at Patch: "He hasn't changed at all, huh?"

"J? Nah," Patch said.

"Kid brother, this is what dorms smell like," Ted said as we rounded the stairs onto the third floor. There was a generic, gray carpet spread all the way down the hall, and as we walked past the many identical doors, I noticed that each one had a white dry-erase board on it. They all had a few colorful notes scribbled on them, like "wanna study at 9?" and "check your e-mail would you?"

Ted stopped in front of a door that had a *lot* of scribbled notes. I quickly surveyed the brightly colored writing—the notes appeared to be largely entreaties for a speedy call back having nothing to do with studying. In fact, a second board had been added below the first for overflow note-leaving. The area all around the dry erase boards was festooned with post-its with little notes encouraging my brother to come meet so-and-so. This would seem to give the impression that my brother had a lot—I mean *a lot*—of friends. Or maybe just . . . admirers?

"You guys ready to be impressed?" Ted asked. "Except Jonathan of course. Jonathan, I don't expect you to be impressed."

He opened the door and we walked into a narrow room with big cathedral windows at the end and two twin beds against opposite walls. In between the windows there was a browning Christmas tree decorated with empty PBR cans. Strung over one of the beds was a canvas hammock, and as we all crammed in behind Ted, we noticed that it was stirring.

"Who's that?" Mickey asked.

"Oh, that's Jed, my roommate."

"Jed *Silbur?*" I couldn't help saying aloud. Jed was this really downtown kid who graduated from Gissing the same year Ted did. He'd started two bands that got record deals before leaving for college, although both of the deals fell through, supposedly because of Jed's problems with authority. And alcohol.

"Yup," Ted said. "Hey Jed, you remember my kid brother, right?"

A guy with a raven-colored mullet peaked out from the hammock. This was another surprise in a long day of surprises. My brother living with Jed Silbur was like Mike Brady rooming with Keith Richards. It was just unreal. It was also unreal how my brother kept referring to me as his "kid brother." Doesn't that sound so . . . assured?

"Hey man," Jed said. He had a really soft voice, but he seemed cogent. At least more cogent than I ever remembered him being in high school. "Hey, Pardo, what's going on? You still playing bass?"

"Nah, gave that up," Mickey said. He was standing in the middle of the room with his arms crossed, and I could tell he was trying to comprehend the Jed-Ted connection, too.

"Oh yeah, you're a big artist now, huh?"

"Or something."

"Hey, that's cool. Listen, I've got to finish my nap, but we're all rocking tonight, right?" Jed nodded at my brother, and then they bumped their fists at each other.

I said yes along with everybody else, because

otherwise I wouldn't have known what to say. I was trying to remember if I'd ever witnessed my brother do anything you could call rocking. Who *was* this Ted guy?

"That's not what I would technically call a cottage," David said, shoving his hands into the pockets of his suit pants.

Mickey nodded his head in agreement, and let out a long whistle.

They were standing at the bottom of a little crest of land, a short walk from the big neo-gothic buildings at the center of campus. At the top of the crest was a well-lit house covered in wisteria that looked like a miniature version of Vassar's imposing main building. Just to be sure, they reread the placard posted at the bottom of the rise, which informed them that this mansion-looking place was, in fact, the President's Guest Cottage.

They had set up beds in the lounge of Lathrop, Ted's dorm (Ted had borrowed sleeping bags from his friends in the Vassar Hiking Club), just in case, but this was looking a whole lot more promising.

David followed Mickey as he leapt up the steps and

snatched the note pinned underneath the ornate, rust-covered doorknocker.

"Blah blah blah, sorry I couldn't meet you, blah blah blah, please make yourself at home, blah blah . . . the campus's newest athletic facility, an Olympic-sized pool, is located, blah blah . . . ," Mickey read. "Cool."

He pushed the door open and walked into a gigantic room with a peaked ceiling, mahogany details, and a stone fireplace that was taller than David. There was a crackling in the fireplace, and they realized that someone had gotten a fire going for them.

"Sweet jeez," said Mickey.

"You better not break anything," David said.

"Ah, man, you've got to get over all these neuroses. What you *meant* to say was that this is a house where we better not *not* have a killer party."

"Okay, you're right," David said. "If we don't have a total blowout party in this house we should go back to New York in shame."

As he said it, he even felt himself mean it a little bit. Mickey had already gone up the stairs—David could hear his feet thumping around on the second floor—and David turned to survey their new accommodations.

The couches and chairs—and there were many of them, set up across the room in various formations that looked conducive to very important sorts of discussions—were made of a dark reddish-brown leather, and there were white fur rugs thrown across several of them. David felt like he had unwittingly stumbled into a Ralph Lauren ad. He threw himself onto the couch closest to the fire—it gave gently and then held him with a reassuring firmness—and then he noticed the bar.

Just to the left of the fireplace there was a collection of cut-glass decanters gleaming with golden liquid. David righted himself and sidled over to the bar, where he poured a healthy portion of something that smelled like burnt rubbing alcohol. He felt five years older just inhaling it, and when he examined himself in the mirror behind the bar, he discovered that it was true: In the red-hand-stained suit, with a tumbler of very old grain alcohol in his hand, he *did* look more sophisticated. Except, of course, for the fact that the hem of his pants was above his ankles, which re-minded him that he wasn't, in truth, very sophisti-cated at all.

"Yo, Davey," he heard Mickey yelling from some-where inside the cottage.

David gave himself one last glance in the mirror and climbed the stairs. After peeking into a series of im-maculately made up rooms, he found the one Mickey was in. There was a large canopy bed with drawn curtains made out of red and gold brocade. On the wall next to the bed there was a plaque. He was stepping toward it when Mickey waved him away.

"It just says the bed was a gift from the Rockefellers—it's originally from Versailles," Mickey, who was standing on the balcony, told him nonchalantly. "What do we have here?" he added, gesturing toward the tumbler.

David handed Mickey the scotch as he joined him on the balcony.

"Whoa," Mickey said. Then he swigged from the scotch, coughing satisfactorily when it was gone. He looked toward David with glassy eyes, but David was looking at something else.

Below them, in the fifty-meter pool that was housed in this remote corner of campus, a group of women in matching black bathing suits and funny white bathing caps were splashing around and making a lot of noise.

"What are those things on their heads?" David said absentmindedly as he watched a pair of perfectly muscled calves break the surface of the pool.

"Well, I was reading in my welcome packet that Vassar was a women's college until 1969—it was one of the, um, six sisters colleges? Anyway, maybe they have some weird former girls' school tradition about wearing old-timey bathing caps."

"Uh, that would be *seven* sisters to you . . . ," David said. He had been half-listening to what Mickey was saying.

"Really? How do *you* know that?" Mickey asked.

"Seven. Definitely seven. Smith, Barnard, Wellesley . . ." David paused and looked at Mickey who was smirking unabashedly. "Shut up."

"David, I just had no idea you were such a proponent of women's higher education. That's awesome."

"I said shut up. And they're playing water polo, you dumbass. Those aren't old-timey bathing caps. They're like special water polo helmets."

"Oh."

They were distracted by some loud screeching and name-calling below. One of the girls seemed to be dragging another girl around by her bathing suit. This went on for a few moments, during which David wasn't sure if he breathed or not. Finally someone blew a whistle and the girls all moved to the edge of the pool for a time-out.

David and Mickey were staring unabashedly when one of the girls noticed them on the balcony. "Hey," she yelled, "are you a professor?"

"Me?" David called down. "Um, no." The girls propping themselves up with their elbows on the side of the pool all started to laugh, but it didn't seem like mean laughing to David. They were all looking up at him, and they all had glowing athletic skin and bright eyes.

50

The tall brunette who had blown the whistle yelled: "Are you an FBI agent?" which caused the girls to erupt again.

"I was just kidding," the first girl went on. "You don't really look like a professor. Or an FBI agent. Especially with that art project on your chest."

David looked down at the red splotches on his shirt, and then at Mickey, who was nodding to himself with satisfaction. "Told you," he said.

"Hey!" One of the other girls exclaimed. "It's that nude photo artist guy."

"Oh yeah," said another. "And that's the cute guy from the photos, too."

"Are you *really* the cute guy from the photos?" said a girl who had pushed herself out of the water and pulled off the cap to release a cascade of bleach-blond hair.

"Um, I guess. One of the guys . . . ," David mumbled, feeling his ears growing hot.

"Oh, I didn't mean to embarrass you," the girl with blond hair said. "I just think you look really good in a too-small suit, too."

David touched his flaming ear and smiled boyishly. It suddenly looked like he didn't have to worry about leaving the attention from girls behind, after all.

"Are you sure this is where we're supposed to meet them?" Arno yelled over "Under Pressure," which was reverberating against the walls of the Mug, Vassar's basement, on-campus bar. That was when he noticed all the glitter-encrusted signs on the walls proclaiming Friday night "Space Disco Night."

"Yeah," Patch said, "hold on a sec." He was texting something, and since he'd only learned to text a week ago, it was taking all his concentration. Patch had insisted on taking an actual tour of the campus, so that he could report back to Greta, and Arno had tagged along.

He still hadn't figured out how he was going to get depth, although he could feel that it must be somewhere nearby. There were *quads* filled with girls out there. Surely some of them had to have depth.

Arno surveyed the scene. Many small cafeterialike tables were set up around the dance floor, which was reflected in the mirrored ceiling. The guy with Buddy

Holly glasses who had served them their beer was currently dancing across the floor—or at least sort of dancing, although the word "hopping" also occurred to Arno. Girls with sparkly eye makeup, frizzed hair, big jewelry, and short-shorts were swaying with guys who had apparently used the sparkly eye makeup, too. It occurred to Arno that a lot of work had gone into Space Disco Night.

He surveyed the girls and tried to imagine taking one of them out for a walk across the quad and a talk about life. He was having a hard time imagining which one of these girls would actually be down for that, though. There were two leggy creatures wearing identical little gold dresses and dancing cheek to cheek, pretty close to them, and though Arno didn't think they looked like the greatest conversationalists, he had to admit they were pretty hot.

"Don't you think Bowie is a genius?" Arno called out to them.

The girls looked back and appraised him. After a long, weird moment passed, Arno realized that he was being ignored.

"Sorry, dude," Patch said, finally putting the phone down and taking a swig of his PBR. "Damn, these things go down quick, huh?"

The two gold-covered girls were paying attention

again. One of them looked at Patch and whispered to the other. Then they both looked at him, and kept dancing, except in a slower, more touching, attention-hungry kind of way.

"I know. Sometimes college kids have no taste," Arno said, crushing his empty can under his foot. He should have known girls like that would care about superficial things, like who *New York* magazine wanted on its cover. "You want another one?"

Patch nodded, and they moved through the crowd of dancers to the bar at the end of the room. A line had formed, and as they joined the end of it, Arno noticed that a girl had replaced the Buddy Holly guy. She had long dark hair that twisted around near her waist, and she was wearing jeans and a wife beater.

"This is pretty cool that they have a campus bar," Patch said.

Arno looked back at the dance floor. Everyone looked like they were having a great time, but Arno tried to concentrate and tell himself that it was all frivolity. *Depth*, he silently reminded himself. That's what he needed.

When they reached the head of the line he smiled at the girl bartender—she was even prettier than he had thought before. She pointed at him and jutted her chin like a person too busy for niceties.

"Two beers," Patch said, laying another bill on the bar.

She reached into a bucket of ice, put two beers on the counter, and took Patch's twenty. As she was counting change out for them, Arno said, "I bet you'd rather be hidden in the library somewhere, reading a French novel."

"Huh?" she said, looking nervously down the line.

"Or studying whatever you study," Arno said. "What do you study? Maybe we could hang out later and talk about it."

She squinted at him. "I don't," she said. "I graduated three years ago. But if you want to get together and talk about how hard it is to get a job with a bachelor's degree from a liberal arts college, I guess I'd be up for that."

"Oh," Arno said, taking his beer and moving slowly away from the bar, "Yeah, maybe I'll come back some night when it's not so busy."

"I'll be here," she barked at him, turning to the next customer.

Arno caught up with Patch, who was walking around the perimeter of the dance floor and who hadn't seemed to notice his friend's botched pickup. "Hey, I wonder what happened to Jonathan and Ted . . ." He twisted his head around to make sure that they weren't some-where in the crowd, and was met instead with the sight

55

of a very large, fratish-looking dude with a flashlight and a plastic badge. He was also yelling.

"Hey!" he shouted at them. "Let's see those armbands!"

"Um, armbands?" Patch looked at him coolly, like a person who has just been spit on and is trying not to be irritated about it.

"Yeah, kiddo, there's no drinking in here if you don't got an armband. And you can't get an armband if you're under twenty-one."

"Well," Patch frowned, "I'm over twenty-one, and I don't have an armband."

This seemed to confuse the guy for a few beats, but then he returned to the idea that an armband equaled ability to drink. "My job is to kick out anyone out who has a beer but doesn't have an armband. And that's just what I'm gonna do," he grunted. Then he grabbed Patch by the wrist and seemed about to pull him out of the bar when a blond girl in converse high-tops and a sleeveless dress that looked like it could also have been a tube-top came skidding up next to them.

"Lou," she squealed excitedly, "you caught him!"

"Who?" asked Lou. He was confused again.

"The *real* Hottest Private School Boy. Can I have him, please?"

"He's underage," Lou said, "At least, I think he is."

"Of *course* he is. He's the HPSB. He's still in high school, duh!" She sighed in exasperation, and turned toward Patch. "I see that you're trying to hide underneath that old baseball hat, but I would have recognized you in a paper bag." The blond grabbed Patch by the hand and pulled him into the crowd on the dance floor. Arno looked up at Lou disgustedly, and realized instantly that he wasn't going to get any sympathy there.

As he was being dragged toward the door, "Rebel Rebel" started up, so Patch couldn't even hear his friend calling for him. Arno felt his mood sink and rise at once. Getting kicked out—that made him an outsider, didn't it? And all outsiders had depth, didn't they?

"Ted's brother!?" squealed the pretty, neo-boho girl my brother had just introduced me to. She had a wide, genuine smile on her face, and she twisted her head left and right so I could give her the double-cheek-kiss treatment. "I can't believe there are *two* of you."

"Naw," Ted said, and to my embarrassment he seemed to be blushing. But then I realized that this was different blushing—not the full-on, please-shoot-me blushing of high school. It was more like his face had just gotten some flattering coloring. "I'm like a paler, very unexciting version of J."

This was the kind of thing I'd been angling to hear by coming to visit my brother, but hearing it now, I was filled with a queasy suspicion that it just wasn't true anymore. I smiled weakly at the girl, trying to show her that I did have some humility. She patted the lush patch of grass next to her.

"I'm Zelda," she said as I sat down in the spot

she had indicated. There were a bunch of other people sitting around on the field, too, smoking cigarettes and looking pretty relaxed for college students at the end of a semester. They were all dressed like Zelda, in loose-fitting peasant gear that looked kind of comfy and expensive at once.

We had been slowly making our way from Lathrop to this campus bar, where everyone supposedly hangs out, but we'd been stopped on the way by a lot of people who wanted to talk to Ted, a surprising number of them hoping he could tell them what was happening that weekend.

So we were running a little late.

Ted sank down on the lawn, and I sat down, too—hesitantly, because grass stains could be potentially disastrous for my jeans—and I smiled at Zelda, who was no longer looking at me. She was carefully pushing Ted's hair behind his ears.

"So how's New York?" one of Zelda's guy friends called out to me. He was wearing a cord vest over a white V-neck shirt and jean shorts. Weird.

"Busy, you know," I said with a shrug.

The guy nodded. "Everyone is so formulaically unconventionally busy there."

"Um, right."

I turned to survey the lawn. Students were

everywhere, walking on the paths that led between the big, brick buildings. Night had fallen, and there was laughter everywhere. Two girls were walking toward me, wearing long, crinkly A-line skirts and silvery collections of bangles on their wrists. They had faces like little foxes, snuggled close to each other, telling secrets. When they had almost reached our group, the one in the belted cardigan, who was wearing her hair in two long braids, dropped her bottom lip in mock horror and yelled, "Get your hands off my boyfriend!"

For a moment I thought she might be referring to me, but then I saw Zelda jump away from my brother. She had been giving him a head massage—at least, that's what it looked like.

"I wasn't . . . ," she began, stammering.

"I know, you goose," the girl with the braids said. She sat down next to Ted, folded her legs up underneath her, and kissed him. The other girl, whose dark hair was arranged in one of those artfully messy ponytails, sat down, too, and gave me a crooked smile.

"I'm Lara," she said. She was sharper looking than the other pink-cheeked girl who was currently rubbing noses with my brother. "I'm visiting for the weekend—that's probably why you don't recognize me."

"Oh yeah? I'm visiting too. Is your high school in the city?"

Lara laughed and put a hand over her mouth. "High school? No, no. I'm visiting from Sarah Lawrence, which isn't *quite* the city."

"Lara, this is my brother, Jonathan," Ted said, looking up from Lara's friend's neck. Lara smiled at me like I was a whole new person. "And J, this is my girlfriend, Margot."

The girl with the long braids leaned forward and kissed me. For a moment I thought she was going to *kiss* kiss me, but then she just gave me the double kiss that seemed to be the clique norm. "It's *so* good to finally meet you," she said. "Ted has just told me so many great things about you."

All I could think of to say was, "Oh, yeah?" because I had never heard of Margot, or even imagined that Ted had a girlfriend. But then, it really *had* been a while since we'd talked. I hoped my mouth wasn't hanging open as I took in the sight of Ted as half of a couple—a really, really good-looking one. Luckily, Margot was still beaming despite my lack of words.

"So, are you going to apply to Vassar?" she asked.

"Maybe—it's really pretty here. And the people seem . . ." I broke off because Margot's face had gone from happy to horrified.

"Jonathan, what are you wearing?"

"Excuse me?"

Everyone in the little circle stared at my feet. I did, too—I couldn't help but think, *yeah, they're garish, but they're not* that *bad*. The silence, meanwhile, continued for an uncomfortably long time.

"Margot's a vegan and really committed PETA person," Ted said gently.

"I mean, are those crocodile?" she said. "Do you know what kind of torture they put those animals through, just to get some flashy shoes?"

"Uh, no . . . I mean no they're not croc. Croc-o-dile." Margot was looking at me in disbelief, but I couldn't help but continue. "They're vinyl, in fact. I only buy vinyl and other, um, non-hide clothing items."

Lara, the girl sitting next to me, let out a long, snide, "Ha!"

Now people outside of their little group were staring, not in an exactly understanding way, and none of them were saying anything. You could've heard a chestnut fall, and I probably would have if I wasn't listening to the blood pumping to my cheeks. Just when this whole silence/staring thing was getting a little ridiculous, Margot tossed her head back and laughed. It was a long, lovely, ringing laugh. I looked around for a reaction, but everyone waited until Margot leaned forward and took me in her arms. Like, actually hugged me, filling my nose with this very pleasant gardenia smell.

"Oh, *Jonathan*," she said, "those are so *obviously* not vinyl."

The group around us sighed and laughed, too. They had a good, long laugh at my expense.

"You can't tell Jonathan what to wear," Ted said with a chuckle. "He takes all of that really seriously."

My embarrassment must have been printed all over my face, because Margot continued, "It's okay, buddy. Even I wear—horror of horrors— fur sometimes. But you should be careful who you buy from, *especially* if you're buying new. There is a lot of cruelty in this world, and we should do our part not to support it, you know?"

Then everyone went back to talking and laughing and loudly enjoying the summer night, but I couldn't help but be flushed by a feeling of total, and very public, lameness.

"Hey man," the guy with the angled bangs and the fitted red-and-white striped T-shirt was saying. Then he said it again, "Hey, uh, hey man."

Patch came to terms with the fact that he wasn't going to be able to ignore this guy much longer. He shook his phone a few more times, as though that might somehow get him service in the bathroom of the basement bar, and then considered throwing it against the wall, before realizing that would mean that he would *never* get to talk to Greta again. Or for the rest of the weekend, at least.

"Hey man," the guy said again. "I know who you are."

Patch resignedly put the phone back in his pocket and looked up. "Hi," he said.

"You're that guy that *New York* magazine wanted to name Hottest Private School Boy," the guy continued excitedly. "I just wanted to say I think that is just camptastic."

"Huh?"

"Like, campy fantastic!" the guy continued. As he spoke, he nervously reformed his bangs so that they crossed his forehead and partially covered his right eye just so. "*And* fascinating. I'm writing my senior thesis on the phenomenon of celebrities who are famous for being famous, like Paris Hilton, you see what I mean? So I really know a lot about this. I actually think it was very savvy of you *not* to have accepted the initial offer to be HPSB. It's sort of like you're hiding your hand a little bit longer, it gives you a certain caché, and it only makes the eventual blowup *that* much more inevitable. I think you have a 95 percent chance of being internationally recognizable by early 2007."

"Wow, could you excuse me?" Patch stepped to his side.

"I understand—laidback and hard to reach is your thing," the guy said. Then he put a hand on Patch's shoulder and looked him in the eye. "Just keep doing what you do so well."

Patch climbed the stairs and pushed his way back through the crowd. He was still sort of pissed that Arno had abandoned him here, especially when Patch-enthusiasm was running so high among the Vassar kids, and when Arno knew he had a girlfriend. Patch decided he was done with this place, and moved—as much as he could, with all the girls reaching out to touch his skin for a brief moment—toward the door. As he slapped a particularly persistent hand away, he realized he felt pretty low—almost as low as those horrible two weeks before he hooked up with Greta again. All this attention was making him feel seriously claustrophobic.

Vassar seemed to offer every cool thing about college except the thing that Patch had been looking forward to most—the chance for him to be anonymous again.

When he reached the door, he was relieved to see Jonathan and Ted descending the stairs. Ted was saying something to the bouncer guy who had tried to kick Patch out earlier—there were handshakes and smiles—and then Jonathan and his brother and a whole bunch of other people entered the noisy, disco ball–lit bar.

"Man, where have you been?" Patch said.

"Sorry dude, it took us forever to get here because my brother knows like every person on campus," Jonathan said. "Check it out, that's Ted's girlfriend."

"No way."

"Yup," Jonathan said, surveying the glittering crowd on the dance floor. "What's going on here? Man, these people are *dressed.*"

"Yeah, I guess it's, like, disco night or something," Patch said.

"Mug rats are usually pretty New Waved-out," Jed Silbur said, pulling up next to Jonathan and Patch with a can of beer for each of them. And with a wink, Jed was dancing across the floor.

"Really glad you finally showed up," Patch said.

"Yeah, it's good to see you, too. Everything okay with Greta?"

Patch shrugged. "She just texted me that she ran into her ex-boyfriend at Stanford."

"Whoa."

"It's not a big deal. I mean, I don't think anything is going to happen. I just want to talk to her, know what I mean?"

"Totally."

"Hey," Patch said, swigging from his PBR. "Where do you think the rest of our friends are?"

"I don't know," Jonathan said. He gave his can of beer a little grimace. "But I sure hope Mickey is preparing for his lecture tomorrow. If the students here can dress this well, they *must* be pretty smart."

Mickey took a long dive, pushing with his arms and legs, froglike, through the water. The night sky was dark, but the underwater lights were illuminating his fellow swimmers. He was surrounded by some fiercely hot legs, treading water on all sides of him, and up above he could hear the muted shouting of some very competitive ladies. He had never played water polo before, much less women's water polo, but he was a quick convert. It was, he knew already, his kind of game.

He had also realized that college was going to be a lot like summer camp, except with more breasts.

He burst through the surface of the pool, lifted his arm, and gave the ball a powerful swat. It sailed into the net. The pool erupted with noise, half of it cheering Mickey's point, the other half enraged by his flagrant disregard for the rules. Mickey only had a few moments to catch his breath before he was tugged back underwater. By the time he emerged again, his boxers were gone.

Kicking his way over to the side of the pool, he looked around for David. He hadn't seen him since roughly the time the girls pulled him into the pool in the first place and assigned him to a team. Mickey pushed himself onto the pool's edge, and there was some giggling over Mickey's lack of a bathing suit. Then Mickey really did start to worry. "Where's my friend?" he shouted loudly.

It took a few moments for the girls to take his questions seriously, and then they all pointed to the house. There was David, sitting on a lounge chair, sipping from an apparently refilled tumbler. He was still wearing the suit, although he had unbuttoned the jacket and loosened the tie. He appeared to be smirking.

"Hey!" Mickey yelled. "Hey Grobart! What, you think you're too good for swimming?"

"Man, I'm just wondering what happened to your panties," David replied, taking a sip of his whiskey.

"C'mon, the water's fine!" Mickey yelled back. When David just shook his head and laughed, Mickey switched tactics. He inhaled a good whiff of chlorine, and shot a conspiratorial look at the girls to his left and right. Their hair was all loose now, and their chests were heaving, catching their breath after the game. The girls treaded water and waited until Mickey gave them the nod. "Get 'im!" Mickey cried.

The girls hurled themselves out of the water, and

made a long, wet dash toward David. That was how Mickey got to see his friend hauled into a swimming pool by fifteen water polo–sculpted college girls. Too-small suit and all.

arno practices going to bed alone

Arno must have worn himself out walking the campus and looking for his guys, because when he half woke up, in the darkened lounge down the hall from Ted's dorm room, he had that dreamy awareness of being asleep. He knew that there was no one else in the room, and he heard a voice in his head—definitely Jonathan's—saying something about the smell. And he knew, even with his brain on autopilot, that the smell wasn't great, and that the carpet that it clung to was possibly as old as he was.

He drifted off again, although it wasn't a particularly restful sleep. Thoughts of superficial college girls who judged guys by the number of times they'd appeared in cheesy magazines danced through his head. He flopped from one side to the other, shifting under the scratchy blanket, which was made of the kind of wool he imagined soldiers slept under if they were stationed in Germany. His dreams were shifting to a battlefield, circa 1942, where the world was very cruel and senseless.

But then bubbling, giggling voices came erupting up the stairs, and a light switched on somewhere near him, and he knew he was going to be awake again.

Now that people were actually near him, he remembered that he'd spent his whole night alone. Wandering. Like a real outsider. He decided to hang onto that feeling a little longer, and continue to be asleep. Or at least pretend to be.

"No, it's really fine," a male voice was saying.

"Are you sure?" That was Jonathan.

"No, little brother, I want you to have my bed," the first voice said in a really sweet tone. Arno realized it was Ted. "And I can sleep at Margot's anyway. You and Patch should stay in my room. It's more comfortable than the lounge."

Arno realized they hadn't even noticed him. He really *was* being left out. They continued talking about what a fun night it had been and what their plans were for the next day, but Arno was too busy concentrating on what an outsider felt like to really listen. That's when he heard the click of high-heeled boots walking past him, and the sigh of the couch across from his. He cracked an eye.

And there was the most beautiful-in-a-meaningful-sort-of-way-looking girl that he had ever seen. She had precise, dark little features, and she was wearing a long skirt and a threadbare tank top that fit her perfectly and was thin enough to show the outline of her light-pink bra. The light from the hall seemed to be glowing on her slender limbs like moonlight. She had all these silver bangles on her wrists, but she was managing not to move them much as she carefully rolled a cigarette.

Arno was acutely aware that his hair, which he had artfully greased earlier in the evening, was now sticking up like crabgrass, and not all of it in the same direction. But he couldn't stop watching as the girl put the hand-rolled cigarette in her perfect little mouth and lit it.

"Lara," another girl called, from somewhere over near Jonathan and his brother.

"Shhh . . . ," said the girl sitting across from Arno. She had a husky voice, even when she was whispering. "There's someone sleeping here."

"Oh," the first girl said. She was giggling. Then she hissed: "C'mon, we're going back to my place. Ted's brother and his friend can sleep here."

"Okay," Lara drawled back. She put the cigarette in her mouth and stood up.

Arno cracked his semi-open eye a little wider and watched as she moved between the ugly dorm furniture toward the hall. When she reached the doorway, she turned back toward him, parted her lips in a sexy smile, and winked.

The morning sunlight streaming through the windows woke David from a dream in which he was being crowned Mister America in a seaside ceremony that involved numerous old-timey bathing beauties, a fleet of FBI men for protection, and an ocean of whiskey. Literally, an ocean of whiskey, although that was also the part of the dream he couldn't remember so clearly. He scratched his bare head and sniffed himself. He smelled of chlorine.

Pushing himself up, he realized that he was on the floor of a really nice room. There were several legs extending from the grand, fluffy bed, and he recognized the short, muscled, non-female ones as Mickey's. He gave himself a little inner nod of satisfaction; this Vassar place was all right. From the numerous, handsome clocks in the room he gleaned that it was a quarter past ten, and from the nervous feeling flowing through his body, he knew that he was up for a reason.

The interview was at eleven-thirty: *That* was why he

was awake so fully and suddenly. He wouldn't have been so nervously anticipating it, except that he was a nervous person born of nervous people, and any sort of rejection was crushing for him. It also occurred to him, as he walked across the shiny, antique-looking floorboards and surveyed the two water polo players who were softly snoring next to his friend, that he probably didn't want to blow his chances of getting into this particular school.

That was when he reached the bathroom mirror and realized that he was wearing boxers, a dress shirt with two red, smeary splotches on the chest, and black mid-calf-high socks. It was not an outfit that recommended his scholarly abilities. His suit jacket was draped over the shower curtain rod. The only item of clothing that hadn't ended up in the pool were his pants (somehow they had been pulled off of him on his way to being tossed into the pool). He found them a few moments later in a bedroom farther down the hall, where two more water polo players slept. At least they smelled more like the Grobart's hall closet than the Vassar pool. But then David remembered how the pants made him look like an overgrown child.

David scratched his head nervously and fought the urge to call his mother and demand that she fix every-thing. Then he took a few slow breaths and told himself that if he expected to get into a top-tier college he better quiet his inner sissy and start thinking creatively.

Forty-five minutes later, David was hustling across the grassy quads of Vassar looking about as preppy-hipster as he ever had. He had found the master bedroom of the President's Guest Cottage, with its clean stock of campus casual wear. The blazer and white V-neck shirt he'd borrowed weren't labels he knew, although he was sure Jonathan did, and as he made his way toward the admissions office in the main building he was keenly aware, for the first time, why people sometimes paid so much for clothes. What he had on now smelled and fit better than anything he'd ever worn in his life.

David didn't feel remotely like a little boy anymore. He felt comfortable and in control, the way athletes were supposed to. He felt a little more like a real man.

By the time he'd sat down in a wood-paneled and book-lined office, opposite a guy dressed more or less exactly as David was dressed (Anson DeLine, Vassar '01), he was feeling pretty confident indeed.

"So you're a ball player?" Anson DeLine asked, clasping his hands and leaning his elbows on his desk so that his face came toward David with a wide, if slightly disingenuous, smile.

"Yeah," David said, "I've played varsity since sophomore year, and I plan to play next year." Anson nodded at him leadingly, so David went on, "And I'd like to play in college, too." He cleared his throat. He had rehearsed this line in his head during the car ride, and now he actually felt bold enough to use it. "But what's really great about basketball is how it's informed the rest of my life, especially my academic life. It's taught me to jump high and hustle, and that's one of the reasons I think I would be the kind of well-rounded person Vassar looks for in prospective students."

Nice, David thought to himself. The interviewer seemed to think so, too. He leaned back in his chair and put his hands behind his head like he and David were old buddies just hanging out at the Eating Club.

"Tell me what you've been reading lately," Anson said.

David's stomach clenched up suddenly. How could he have been so *stupid* as to not have anticipated this question? He opened his mouth to mumble something about *Madam Bovary*, which he was reading for his English class, when there was a loud noise from the hall. It sounded like a door being slammed, and then slammed again several more times. David's interviewer look alarmed, and when he jumped up and headed toward the hall to see what was happening, David followed behind him.

The door to the office next to the one they had been sitting in was indeed being slammed, repeatedly. The person doing the slamming was a miniature blonde in a tiny miniskirt and oversized sweater, and David knew immediately that it was Sara-Beth Benny, the child star whom his friends had hung out with on the educational cruise they'd taken last winter. He knew (because Jonathan had told him) that she partied a lot in New York, and also that she was always on the verge of breaking down.

"Susan, are you okay?" Anson called over Sara-Beth's shoulder to the person yelling from behind the door. David was suddenly reminded of his interview and decided that diffusing this situation might be a good recovery from the fumbled book question.

"Hey, Sara-Beth," he said gently. She ignored him and continued slamming the door. Then he stepped closer, slipped his arms around her waist, and gently pulled her back. To his surprise, she didn't fight him. Instead, she collapsed against his chest and began to sob. "Hey," he whispered, looking apprehensively at his interviewer and the woman who had come out from behind the door.

"I'm so glad you're here," Sara-Beth said between teary gasps. David paused and tried to think how to take this. He had just been hoping she would remember him at all, but the touchy friendliness they were engaging in now was definitely without precedent.

"Um, you too," he said, trying not to sound surprised. "Are you okay?"

"No!" she shrieked.

The two interviewers looked at David expectantly. "What happened?" asked David.

"This moo-cow, she . . . she . . ." Sara-Beth started sobbing again, and for a moment it seemed like she wasn't going to be able to finish her sentence. David took the opportunity to inhale the vanilla smell wafting up from her heaps of multihued blond hair. "They asked me to do the routine."

"What routine?" David said. He realized immediately that this was probably the wrong thing to say, but he was just glad that his mouth was still able to form words.

"You know, the opening dance routine from *Mike's Princesses*."

"Oh."

Mike's Princesses, the show Sara-Beth started acting in when she was six years old, began with a song and dance routine in which she and her two fictional older sisters introduced themselves and their basic personality traits. It was very show-tuney and, even to a bunch of second graders, very obviously lame. It ended with Mike's swinging all the girls around until they squealed, and then kissing them on the forehead.

Sara-Beth whimpered into David's borrowed white

V-neck as he turned to look at the two interviewers. The funny protective feeling he was feeling toward her must have shown on his face, because the woman named Susan gave him this apologetic look and plaintively said, "I'm a fan."

This elicited a loud sob from Sara-Beth, and she took a fistful of David's shirt.

"Well, I really don't think that's very appropriate," David said. He could feel Sara-Beth nodding vigorously into his chest. He cleared his throat and raised his voice. "Or very classy." The interviewers stepped back. They did actually look sort of chastised. David moved away from them toward the entryway, half supporting, half dragging Sara-Beth. He wondered briefly if the clothes were transforming him into a more confrontational person, but before his doubts could slow him down he was saying, "And, come to think of it, there's no way I could consider attending a school like Vassar where stuff like this is allowed to happen!" He had the door open, and he and Sara-Beth were practically out of there. The interviewers were staring at them, mouths agape.

Sara-Beth didn't let go of David until they were safely outside, with the quiet campus all around them. "Thank you," she whispered.

"It was nothing," David said. "I just feel bad for you."

"No, you don't understand," Sara-Beth said as she picked up his hand and squeezed it. "Arno, no one's ever done anything remotely like that for me before."

Um, *Arno?*

"I find your work especially courageous," said the chair of the Vassar Art department. "I mean this conflagration of talent is so rare, especially in an artist so young."

The chair, Brenda Breton, dragged her fingers across Mickey's knee as she spoke. They were sipping Sancerre in a small room, which Professor Breton had several times referred to as the *salon*, adjacent to the lecture hall. The room did have silk upholstered chairs and wall sconces, which did seem kind of elegant to Mickey. Despite the fact that she was well over forty, the professor's cleavage was smooth and tremendous. Mickey, who was wearing a vintage Charlie's Angels shirt and David's little kid suit pants, was finding it difficult to concentrate.

"Thanks," he said.

"How are you liking the cottage?" asked the auburn-haired woman sitting in the sofa chair on Mickey's other side. She appeared to be a few years younger than

Professor Breton, and her name was Lourdes. Professor Lourdes Soto of nearby Sarah Lawrence college, who specialized in postmodern art movements. She was wearing a flowing, fashionable dress that Mickey found surprising on an academic.

"It's sweet," Mickey said.

"Usually Brenda has me stay there when I visit, but I guess she thought you were more important," Professor Soto said, smiling conspiratorially and fluffing her sable bob.

"Oh, hush, Lourdes. You know it's only because I like having you stay in my house," Professor Breton said.

"But I can't say I disagree about your importance," Professor Soto went on. "We're all very impressed by the attention you've managed to garner already."

"Seems like there's enough room in that cottage for both of us," Mickey said, winking at Professor Soto and taking a healthy gulp of wine. "It's pretty phat."

"Mmmm . . . ," Professor Soto said. "You know, we have lovely grounds, too."

"You mean at Sarah Lawrence?" Mickey asked, remembering his earlier poolside conversation with David. "That's one of the seven sisters, too, huh?"

"Why, yes," Professor Breton said, gesturing to the grad student who had been darting in and out of the room to refill her wine. "It's quite grand, although I think you may find our modest *salon* more comfortable." She waved a hand at their low-lit surroundings. The walls were decorated with many romantic landscape paintings, several of them featuring big, moody clouds, hung in gigantic gold-leaf frames.

"My colleague is *too* modest," Professor Soto said icily. She reached over and brushed something off Mickey's shoulder, letting her fingers linger there. "But Sarah Lawrence has its charms. It was a private mansion originally, you know, so it is more intimate than Vassar."

"No kidding," Mickey said.

"Perhaps you would like to come and see it?" she said.

"That would be awesome. I mean, I'm leaning toward applying to art school next year, but I want to see as many schools as I can."

"Mickey, you've got to stop talking like that. Art school! You're a *real* artist now," Professor Breton said, leaning close enough to him that he could smell her heavy perfume. Mickey felt like Fergie had just told him he could really dance.

"I hate to admit this," Professor Soto chimed in, "but she's right. You're a hot ticket. In fact . . . would you consider giving a lecture at my college?" she said slowly, as though it had just occurred to her. "Our speaker for next Saturday cancelled, and it would be a major coup to have a Pardo at the lectern."

Professor Breton choked on her wine. "He doesn't lecture for free, you know," she said sharply.

"Oh, we'll take care of him," Professor Soto said, rubbing Mickey's shoulder again.

Mickey could almost *feel* his career taking off. He just hoped that the friendship between the two hot professors didn't get destroyed in the process. Luckily the grad student who had been pouring their wine reappeared before either of them said anything too mean.

"Everyone's seated, Professor," she said. "You want to go on in five?"

"Excellent, darling," Professor Breton replied, waving the grad student away. "So, Mickey, I've prepared a glowing introductory speech . . ."

"Professor Breton *always* gives good glow," Professor Soto said.

By the time the grad student returned, Mickey was feeling pretty good about his prospects for wowing just about anybody.

They stood up and walked across the Persian rug toward the door to the lecture hall. Professor Breton, right behind him, rested her hand on Mickey's shoulder and whispered, "I am going to compare you to Gauguin in your artistic quest for freedom and unique understanding of the human form."

"Really? Cool," Mickey said.

"Yes," she said. "What have you prepared?"

"Well, I gave my slides to that grad student person," he said. "But really, I was thinking more I'd just freestyle it." Which was clearly a brilliant idea.

i am on the outside of cool, looking in

Just for the record, I am not a bad person.

I mean this whole thing with my brother Ted being well-adjusted, much-adored, and possessed of a beautiful girlfriend is great. I really think so. It just took a few hours and a few beers and, okay, a good night of sleep to wrap my mind around the new state of affairs.

But by Saturday afternoon, I was finding my brother's lifestyle changes more interesting than personally threatening. So I asked him if he wanted to spend some quality family time, and then we'd catch Mickey's lecture a little late. This request seemed to impress Ted and make him happy, and as soon as it was out of my mouth I knew that I'd done the right thing by not being upfront with him. My plan was to find a delicate way to ask him if he was drinking a new brand of bottled water, or was perhaps the subject of some college sleep test where they inject you with coolness, but he didn't need to know that's what I was getting at. Of course, this was a goal made slightly less attainable by the continued presence of Margot.

The three of us were walking across campus, in the fading warmth of afternoon, to have a late lunch at some diner in town. Mickey's lecture was supposed to be starting in half an hour, and I was surprised by how many people seemed to be streaming toward it already.

A somewhat androgynous guy-girl couple in black-rimmed glasses, paint-splattered white T-shirts and Carhartt work jackets were passing us, and as they did I caught a whiff of turpentine and smoke.

"Don't all these people look sort of the same?" I couldn't help but ask.

Margot laughed and tossed one of her braids over her shoulder. "Yeah, that's what art students look like in Vassarland."

As we came to the edge of campus, I saw a group of guys sitting under a tree. They were all wearing blazers and sweaters over collared shirts and nubby, faded brown shoes. They also emanated a distinctive smell.

"Are those pipes they're smoking?"

"Yeah," Margot laughed. "Those guys are all Professor Connor's advisees. He's like this ancient, quasi-famous literary critic who teaches this postwar American lit class that is impossible to get into. They're all really, really into being English majors."

"Wow."

"That's what college is like—there are more options, and people are more creative. But basically it's just as tribal as high school," Ted said.

"Huh," I said. "So what tribe are you a part of?"

Margot was holding Ted's hand, and he was sort of stroking it. She laughed again, which was a good thing—I was really starting to like her laugh. "Oh, Ted's not part of a tribe. He belongs to everybody."

Ted looked at me seriously. "That's sort of true—I have a really diverse group of friends. But to be totally honest, from outside looking in, I think I probably fit a type, too."

Margot leaned in toward me and stage-whispered, "Ted is always *totally honest*, by the way."

"No kidding," I stage-whispered back.

"I'm being serious, though," Ted said, gratuitously. "Like, people are always calling me 'do-gooder Ted,' and I know what they mean when they say that. Like a bunch of Margot and my friends, I try to be in the world in a nondetrimental way, and I'd like to do some good for other people. So, that's my tribe, I guess."

Yes, my brother does actually speak this way. Although it seems a lot less silly coming from a guy who has a girl like Margot stroking his arm.

Soon we were sipping milk shakes and eating fries at a booth in an authentic old-fashioned diner. "It's weird," I said, "there are so many places in New York that just hurt themselves straining to look like this place. But you can tell they've just been doing the same old thing for like a quarter of a century or something."

And then, since things were feeling very familial, even with Margot there, I went ahead and asked. "Ted, man, tell me what's changed in you. It's like you're the same, but different too."

"That's a tough question, J," he said, furrowing up his brow and looking at me like he was about to explain the causes of third world poverty or something.

"I just mean that I'm really into your scene up here. It seems like you have awesome friends. Big stuff is happening for you. It's really nice to see that." I paused for a moment, and then realized that my comment might have sounded a little cruel. "Not that you didn't have awesome friends or big stuff in the city."

"But I didn't really," Ted said. "I'm going to tell you something—but don't let it go to your head. When I first got here, I realized that college is like this crazy chance to be a whole new person. You have to make new friends, and get new interests, and there's virtually no one around to call you out as a poseur. So I decided I was going to be that New York cool kid who always goes back to the city on weekends for the night life and drinks black coffee and spends all day planning his night on his cell phone. Basically I wanted to be you."

"But I don't drink my coffee black . . . ," I said in a very small voice.

"That's not the point. Or maybe it is. Nobody bought my act, because it wasn't me. I realized that if I was going to have friends and be happy, I was going to have to be confident about my *real* self. So that's what I did, but more so—I'm the guy who cares, and I don't mind everybody knowing that," Ted said. "And what I found out was, if you're not hiding your face all the time, people really like that guy. Caring *is* cool."

"Wow," I said.

"You might find this all hard to believe," Margot said, "because high school can be such a shallow time. But a guy who cares is hot. To care is *unbelievably* sexy."

"And that's who I always was anyway," Ted said. Then he did finally laugh a little bit. "So I lucked out."

"Wow," I said again, and gave myself a moment of quiet contemplation to take this all in. When I looked up, Margot and Ted were silently gesturing at me to look over my shoulder.

When I looked, I saw a dark-haired guy feeding small bites of grilled-cheese sandwich to a blonde in big movie-star shades. I knew immediately that the blonde was Sara-Beth Benny, but it took me another moment to realize that the guy was my friend David.

As he cut another piece of sandwich with his knife and fork, I heard her ask, "Are you absolutely positive it's okay to eat carbohydrates after two in the afternoon? My trainer said that . . ."

Then I turned back to Margot and my brother, trying not to laugh, and I saw that she had her forehead rested against his, and their lips were almost touching. Suddenly, I felt a little bit sad. I missed doing things like going to the movies or old-fashioned diners with Flan—or maybe just with a girlfriend.

I glanced at David and Sara-Beth again, and saw that they were now mid-nuzzle, and then back at my brother, but he and Margot were rubbing their noses together in a really intimate way. I rested my eyes on my greasy fries and sucked the last clumps of milk shake from my glass.

That's when I decided I was just going to have to find a way to follow Ted's advice. If I could find a way to care about *something*, maybe I could have a smart and gorgeous girlfriend to feed bite-sized pieces of sandwich to, too. I mean, that sounds reasonable, right?

Right.

"Mickey!" Arno yelled over the crowd. "Yo, Mickey freaking Pardo!"

The noise around him was intense, however, and there were a lot of people between him and his friend. It felt like his cries were being swallowed up by the crowd. And even though he was being pushed along on a stream of people like he was just anybody, Arno was feeling much less sorry for himself.

He was still feeling the sickly sweet triumph of being treated like a total outsider the night before. Plus, he had changed into new clothes, which had reminded him that he was only wearing a specific shade of lightly faded black these days, and how cool that was. If he wasn't deep yet, he felt confident that he was getting pretty damn close.

And also, he had just watched one of his oldest friends lecture to a crowd of college art students and teachers. The lecture had gone unbelievably well. Now girls were running circles around Mickey, who was being carried on one of these ancient Aztec chairs that apparently had been on display in the lecture hall's small anthropology museum.

The whole hoopla was bound to reflect positively on Arno. He thought momentarily that perhaps that wasn't his deepest of moments, but then brushed the idea away. Was that girl taking her shirt off right in front of Mickey? Wow.

When he finally caught up to Mickey, his friend jumped off the chair and let out a war whoop in greeting. He was wearing a huge feather headdress that definitely looked like it belonged in a glass case.

"Good job, man," Arno said.

"You think they bought it?" Mickey grinned back.

"You could say that," Arno said. "I mean, the fact that there was a spontaneous striptease happening on stage is a pretty positive sign, don't you think?"

All around them, girls were pulling off pieces of clothing and dancing. It reminded Arno of that Greek play he'd read for his literature class—the one where all the women get wasted and pull down a tree with their hands.

"Who knew you could inspire such mayhem, dude," Arno said. Then someone ran by and told them about a keg that was being set up behind some hall or other.

Mickey's eyes got all red and swirly, and he threw back his head and yelled, "To the beer, dudes!"

By the time Arno had located the keg, there was music blaring from the open windows of the dorms and a line of people, excitedly rehashing the lecture, had formed. They were making a lot of loud, joyously nonsensical noises, too. Arno had lost Mickey again, but he got in line anyway—he figured once he had beer in his hands Mickey would reappear instantly.

It wasn't until he was next in line that he noticed the slender girl with the dark ponytail. She must have been standing in front of him the whole time. She was wearing tight jeans tucked into pirate boots and a shimmery tunic thing and she was bending over the keg. It took Arno several moments to realize that she was the same gorgeous girl from his half-dream last night.

"Need some help?" he said, feeling suddenly like this might be destiny.

She looked back and smiled at him like she knew he would be there. Without saying anything, she stood gracefully and handed him her cup. Arno leaned over and exaggerated the motion of beer pumping, until he had four plastic cups full. The girl waited for him, and when he was done, they walked down the slope together, holding their drinks out in front of them so as not to spill a drop.

"*That* was embarrassing," she finally said, as she sat down on the grass. She shook her head so that her ponytail danced against her back. They way she did it made Arno think that she wasn't embarrassed at all.

"Nah," Arno said, sitting next to her. "I've known lots of girls who have that problem."

She lifted her eyebrows as she took a sip of foamy beer and looked at the mayhem. "The thing is, I never drink beer."

"Yeah, I've heard girls say that before, too."

"It's not that I don't appreciate beer, and I'm not, like, frightened of the calories like most girls," she explained, taking another sip of foam. "It's just that when I drink, I prefer the wine my parents make."

"*Make?*"

"Well, you know, *produce*. My parents own a vineyard in Napa. It's gorgeous, and their pinot noir has a really elegant taste. They named one of their champagnes Lara, after me."

Arno wasn't sure how something could taste elegant, but he liked the way she put a dramatic emphasis on the words *gorgeous* and *champagne*. It made her sound vaguely European. Also, she was even prettier than she had appeared last night, so he just nodded and said, "Must be really beautiful out there."

"Scorched hills, heavy vines. It's like paradise. I wish I could be there all the time, and just like, till the soil."

"You don't like college?"

"I like it fine, I just wish it were more about lectures and brilliant ideas. Everyone thinks that college is about *entertaining* us these days and . . ." She sighed. "It's just a lot of bullshit, sometimes, you know? Like living in a small town where everyone is the same age and has the same interests. And I don't even go here— I'm just visiting from Sarah Lawrence. And if you think this is a small school, you should check out mine."

"Yeah, there's a lot of conformity out there," he said.

"You must know all about that."

"Sure, I mean . . . wait, what are you trying to say?"

"Oh, you know, Arno Wildenburger, Hottest Private School Boy. Everyone loves you when you have a title," she said with a delicate shrug of the shoulders. "I didn't mean to bring up a painful topic. I just mean, I know *you know* what I mean."

Arno nodded, and tried to convince himself that he knew exactly what she meant, although all he could really think about was the fact that she already knew who he was. That had to mean something, right? Arno paused to survey the shrieking, churning, quasi-clothed undergrads. It was dusk, and the girls were dancing on any raised surface they could find. It made him feel sort of sorry for them.

"I have witnessed a lot of really callous behavior,"

Arno said. "Sometimes I feel like I'm surrounded by . . . kids, you know?"

"No one really grows up until they've been in love," Lara replied, doing the shrug thing again, like she was a girl who'd really been out there and lived hard.

Arno turned and looked into her exotically dark eyes. "Well, maybe I could be in love with you."

She rolled her dark eyes and released an impatient sigh. "Maybe you can find me once you've tried it out on someone else."

Arno realized that her statement had multiple interpretations, but he decided to go with the one that favored him the most. "I saw you in my dreams last night," he said, meaningfully.

Lara turned and looked at him with a serious and unreadable expression. She stared at him longer than people usually stare in real life, as though she were searching for something inside him, and then she took a lollipop from behind her ear. She didn't take her eyes from him as she unwrapped it. Then, instead of licking it, she bit into it. Arno stared at the slight parting of her lips until it started to drive him crazy. So he went for it.

They shared warm, candy-flavored kisses for a long time, on the slope, oblivious to the chaos all around them.

Patch was back from his hike.

He had found the highest point on campus, which had finally made his cell phone work. It hadn't made him able to talk to Greta, however, as hers was either out of juice or turned off. He'd checked his messages—just one, in which Greta said many things that were drowned out by all the people in the background. He hadn't wanted to think about it until now, but Greta had told him once about her first serious boyfriend, who was a senior back when she was a freshman, and who, he was pretty sure, went to Stanford now. And now Greta—the only girl he's maybe even . . . *loved* . . . was 3,000 miles away with her ex-boyfriend. It was killing him.

Patch shoved the phone in his pocket and walked back to the center of campus, where bonfires were burning and everyone seemed to be enjoying themselves. *Really* enjoying themselves. Really loudly.

He walked up to a group of girls who were dancing to the MIA song playing on their boom box, and asked them if they'd seen the kid who had just given the lecture. "He's my friend, but I was a jackass and I missed it," he added.

The girls looked like pretty normal college girls, if a little sorority-esque with their straight blond hair and their tans, but apparently they weren't normal, because as soon as they saw Patch they started jumping up and down and whispering "Oh my god," into their hands.

"It's the HPSB," one of them said, her voice quavering.

"It totally is."

"Can I just say, you look *so hot* without your clothes on?"

"Um." Patch fiddled with the phone in his pocket.

"Do you just wear that old baseball cap so people won't recognize you?"

"You shouldn't—you're gorgeous."

"So, like, who's the redhead? Because you don't seem like the marrying type."

Patch was overwhelmed by the questions, and displeased with their direction. He was trying to think of a graceful exit when a big hand slammed into his shoulder and he went flying forward into the circle of girls.

"Sorry," he said, righting himself. The girls hadn't seemed to mind.

"Katy, why the hell don't you have your shirt on?"

the big guy with the big hand said. Patch suddenly realized that the girls weren't wearing swimsuits. They weren't at the beach, after all, and what they had on was now looking a lot more like bras and panties.

"Excuse me," Patch said, going back over to the Pusher. He was wearing his visor upside down and sideways, his shirt said TKE, and even though he was shorter than Patch, his arms looked like they knew their way around a weight room. "But that was weak."

The Pusher thought this over. "I ain't weak."

"As in lame. Uncool. Uncalled for."

The Pusher's friends were gathering round, muttering. "What the hell is going on here?" one of them said. The girls had stopped dancing, and they were watching the frat dudes apprehensively.

"It's a freakin' skin show."

"Hey, is that our keg?"

"Who's that little freak drinking right out of it?"

"Um," Patch said again, because he knew without looking that the little freak was Mickey. "Listen, dudes . . ."

"Oh, yeah? Why should we listen to the Hottest Private Whatever when clearly all he wants to do is steal our women, get 'em drunk and make 'em take their clothes off?"

Patch scratched at his forehead. "Dude, I respect the

fact that you are the only guys who are allowed to do that." He had always been lucky enough to sound sincere even when was going for sarcasm. "But it's just a party. Everyone's just having a good time."

"Yeah, you're having a good time because my girlfriend doesn't have her shirt on," the Pusher yelled in Patch's face. "I'm gonna go kick that freak's ass and shut this party down. And when I'm done with that, I'm gonna take care of you."

Patch breathed deeply, and let the Pusher see the whites of his eyes.

"Dude. Would you listen to me? I get it. My girlfriend is, as we speak, unreachable and partying in California. Do you know how that makes me feel? Any idea?"

The Pusher thought about this. "A little bit."

"You have a little bit of an idea? Because I really wouldn't care if your girlfriends were all topless right now. Buck naked. I'd trade it all just to get a *call* through to my girl."

The Pusher and his backup frat guys seemed kind of touched by this.

"The best I can do," Patch said, "the best that *I* can do right now, is party. Be a part of the party, and not ruin anybody else's party. You know what I mean?"

The frat guys all hung their heads for a minute, and

then collectively pumped their fists in the air. There was a long silence, and then the Pusher said, "That was beautiful, man. Let's party!"

The guys continued to whoop and cheer, and Patch, still fiddling with the cell phone in his pocket, went off to pry Mickey from the keg.

Before he could do that, though, he spotted Jonathan, and the scene was weird enough that he had to pause and make sure it was actually him. It was. He was sitting on the grass next to a petite blonde who was wearing a conservative, navy blue suit, pearl studs, and two large circular pins on her chest that proclaimed *Bush/Cheney 2004* and *Campus Republicans*. She was vigorously pounding her little fist into her other little palm.

"Marriage means one man one woman, end of story," Patch heard her say.

"Wow," Jonathan said, apparently without irony. "So that's what you care about."

"Yes, and the thing about me—as opposed to the liberals who run this campus—is that I really *do* care. It's not just a smarmy front. I care *a lot*."

"Excuse me," Patch said. The girl looked up with this don't-tick-*me*-off kind of expression, but as soon as she saw Patch her piercing gaze softened. "I think this guy needs to take a breather. Can I borrow him from you?"

"Oh, okay," she said, blushing. Jonathan jumped up and shook hands with the girl.

"Thanks, Pam," he said. "I don't think I agree with you, but seeing your passion . . . well, that really helped a lot."

As they headed in the direction of Mickey, who was still attached to the keg, Jonathan turned to Patch and said, a little crazily, "I had no *idea* there were so many things to care about."

that old thing that's been pumping in arno's chest all these years

Arno found himself standing on the bottom of the slope again. He was holding two fresh beers—one for Lara and one for him. The grassy expanses of the Vassar campus had been overwhelmed by the kind of partying that only happens with just the right combination of heat, hormones, and Mickey Pardo. It was loud and salty out there.

But Arno didn't really care about any of that. What he cared about—a lot, and suddenly—was that Lara girl. And where she had disappeared to.

He blinked his eyes. Surely something was amiss here. He had just been telling Lara about his parents' art gallery and how awesome it was to go there at night to look at art by himself. Or with a girl.

Arno was reasonably sure that conversation had gone deep.

He surveyed the masses of people, who were dancing and shouting and showing off their skin. Even with most of the girls stripped down to their bras, caroming around on dudes' shoulders, the only thing he wanted to see was the girl with the dark eyes and sparkly top.

The beers in his hands now looked sad. What was he going to do with them without her?

Then he remembered what she'd said. Before he could have a meaningful relationship with a girl like Lara, he was going to have to have already been in love. Arno took a sip of one beer, and then the other, and wondered if he could wait.

There was a feeling growing in his chest. It was a rare kind of sadness, almost a little bit like pain. He looked down there, just to make sure everything was okay, and he realized that his heart was beating like crazy. He could actually feel it pumping this bizarre, unfamiliar pain/pleasure feeling all over his body.

And then he knew what the feeling was. It was love. Love was beating in his heart.

my friends *are* the afterparty

It was nearly dawn, and my friends and I were splayed out on luxurious leather couches in perhaps the largest room you could possibly describe as *cozy*. This was the "cottage" that Mickey had neglected to show me till like two hours ago—the one the Vassar Art Department had seen fit to put him up in. Apparently, it had been worth their while. Mickey Mania was currently sweeping the campus. For my part, I was just really enjoying the whole fireplace, scotch, country-chic thing.

"Hey, you guys want to do this again next weekend?" Mickey said, tossing his cell over his head and not catching it as it came falling down on the hearth. He picked it up and looked at it for a minute, but I guess it must have still been working okay, because he flipped it open and started playing cell phone Deer Hunter.

"Hell yes," Arno said. He said it sort of dreamily, though. Apparently he had met and become smitten with Margot's friend, Lara. Which figures—Arno usually only falls for girls who are as absurdly good-looking as he is and know it. So I guess that explains the starry eyes. "How are we going to do that?"

"Argh!" Mickey was keying into his cell furiously. "Hold on. Hah! Die! What? Oh, yeah. Let's do this again next weekend!"

"Right. How are we going to do that?" I said.

"This professor I met before my lecture? She was really impressed. She says the speaker she was going to have next Saturday at *her* college just cancelled and she said—get this—a Mickey Pardo lecture would be a *major coup.*"

"Shut up," Patch said. He shook his head in that very Patch unbelieving-but-heard-it-all-before way. "I can't believe I missed this lecture of yours."

"It was wild," Mickey said.

"You should have seen our boy," Arno said. "He had this laser pen, and he was like pointing at different people's bodies and talking about the modulation of color on nipples and shit. It was hilarious!"

"So this professor said that Vassar is like sixty percent female, but her college—Sarah

Lawrence—is like *seventy-five* percent," Mickey said. "Ya'll will go with me now, right?"

"Just so long as we get to stay in the President's Guest Cottage, or whatever the equivalent is," I said.

"Professor Soto *did* say that the campus used to be a private estate with like mansions on it and stuff," Mickey said. "I guess that's how it got its name—Sarah Lawrence was the founder's old lady."

"Wait, did you say Sarah Lawrence?" Arno looked like he was the hero in a costume drama and he was about to run across a field of wildflowers to embrace his mistress. His face was that lit up.

"Uh, yeah," Mickey said, squinting his eyes at Arno like he was slow or something. "Sarah Lawrence. Private estate. Seventy-five percent female."

"*Lara* goes to Sarah Lawrence," Arno said. "And I was actually thinking that might be a really good place for me next year. Like, maybe I could apply early action and . . ." We all watched him drift with the wildflowers for a moment. Eventually, mercifully, he snapped out of it. "Man, that was one wild party."

"Yeah," I said, hoping the conversation would *not* return to Lara. There was something cruel about her that I couldn't quite pinpoint, and even though Arno has done wrong many more times than he's *been* done wrong, I still sometimes feel a little protective of him. Which is absurd, I know. "I always thought college social life was going to be sort of underwhelming, after New York and everything, but that was like, pretty bacchic. I mean, do you even realize what just happened to that campus?"

"It was pretty crazy."

"That was the most fun I've had in weeks."

"Totally."

We all paused and thought about that, soaking in the high-end hunting lodge ambience, sipping our drinks.

"Wouldn't it be sweet if we all ended up going here?" Mickey said.

We all murmured our agreement, because we all realized at once how *cool* that would be— starting over, but having your best people with you.

"Hell yeah," Arno said. "It seems like there's just so much to experience here. I mean, college is going to totally give us so much depth."

I couldn't believe I'd just heard Arno use the D word, but I had to nod because I kind of felt the same way. Even if it sounded cheesy, wasn't that sort of what I wanted, too?

"College is going to be awesome," Mickey went on, and we all just laughed and said hell yes, and didn't mention the irony that it was Mickey—the worst student among us—who was getting excited about college.

"I don't know, man," Patch said, after a pause, "I mean it's been hella fun being here with you guys, and that party was all right. But maybe Vassar's too close to home, you know? Culturally, I mean. Like everyone already knew who I was here. It made me feel . . . *bad*."

"I mean, maybe not *here* here," Mickey went on. "But you know, all of us at the same school, living in weird housing, copying each other's home-work—that'd be pefect!"

I smiled, because it really did sound just about perfect, but Patch still didn't look sure. "I know you and Greta really want to go to the same school," I said. "You think you can convince her to go to an East Coast school?"

And then Patch gave me that wide, sparkly smile that makes people just topple for him. "Sure," he said. "That's the way it's gotta be." Then he muttered, "It's *gotta*," again, kind of quietly.

So everything seemed pretty okay right then—my friends were all together, taking advantage of the good things, and we were having our horizons super expanded. We had this big chance to remake ourselves as better people just a year away, but *with* each other. All of us together: me, Mickey, Arno, Patch, and . . .

"Hey guys?" I said, sitting up in my cushy armchair. "When was the last time any of you saw David?"

"Do you have anything to eat?" David asked.

It was five in the morning and he was sitting on one of the geometrical, all-white pieces of furniture in Sara-Beth Benny's apartment, back in the city. Everything in the room that wasn't white was metallic with clean, straight lines. The apartment was also really high up, in one of the tall, shiny black Trump buildings, and most of the walls were made of glass. David was afraid of going too close to the windows, so he had parked himself in the middle of all this whiteness. It was the coldest-feeling space he had ever been in, and even though he wasn't remotely hungry, he thought that putting some hot food inside him might help.

"Eat?" Sara-Beth said, her forehead shrinking a little and her eyes getting kind of wide. She was wearing a white, spaghetti-strap dress that looked sort of prairie-like. It accentuated all her childlike qualities.

"Um, maybe breakfast or something? It was a long drive back from Vassar."

Sara-Beth's driver had driven them back to the city, but it had taken much longer than usual because she kept complaining that her stomach was upset and insisting that they pull over. David was relieved that she never actually threw up, although the driver said something cryptic implying that it wouldn't be the first time.

"There's no food here," Sara-Beth said finally, the blue of her eyes growing more intense as she spoke.

"Nothing?" David said. "Maybe we should get out of here, then."

"You want to get out of here?" She looked so full of emotion that she might burst. "Why? I mean, I told you I was sorry for calling you Arno."

"We, I said *we*," David said gently. He would have wrapped this girl up in his arms and squeezed her with all his might if he weren't so afraid of breaking her. "And it's okay about the Arno thing. Sometimes I wish I were Arno, too."

"Really? Then you understand me. I can't tell you how many times a day I wish I were somebody else." Sara-Beth's faced crumpled and a tear slid down her cheek. "You're the *only one* who understands me, David, and now you want to leave . . ."

"I don't want to leave *you*. It's just that . . . don't take this the wrong way, but your apartment kind of freaks me out. It's really cold in here."

"I know!" Sara-Beth wailed. "It's horrible. My mom insisted I have this famous interior decorator do it so that *W* magazine would do a piece about me and my apartment and now all I can think about is what if I spill something or someone comes over with dirt on their shoes and . . ." Sara-Beth stopped talking—she was sobbing so hard that she couldn't get any more words out.

"I understand that," David said, coming over and sitting next to her on the long white couch and taking her little hand in his. "I think this place is really unfriendly, especially for a girl living by herself."

"Mm-hmm," Sara-Beth managed through tears. David stroked her back as she began to calm down. Finally, when the tears had stopped, she turned her face up to him. Her lips were trembling, and her eyes were still that intense blue color. It was visually stunning, and he had a front row seat. "Sometimes I wish I could just throw myself through all that glass," she said dramatically.

"Don't even talk like that," David said. He was wondering if maybe he'd inherited the therapy gene from his parents, because all he wanted to do right then was make this girl feel safe. "I think this place is really unhealthy for you. I think you should get out of here, and as soon as possible."

"But I can't even picture living anywhere but

here . . . ," she wailed. "I'm like a bird, and this apartment is my cage."

"But you could go anywhere! There are so many different kinds of places to live. Like, take my parent's apartment in the Village—it's probably a quarter of the size of this place, but it feels cozy and lived in, you know?"

"I love the Village," Sara-Beth said, sniffling. "Is your apartment near the Magnolia Bakery?"

"Um, kind of . . ."

"David," Sara-Beth said, pushing herself up onto his lap and fixing her now-dry eyes on his. "Let me come live with you."

A few hours and a lot of talking later, David and Sara-Beth were in the Grobart's kitchen, whispering so as not wake up his parents. Sara-Beth was still wearing the white dress, but now she was also wrapped up in David's Potterton sweatshirt. She looked especially tiny in it; he couldn't stop looking at her.

David had considered Jonathan's advice about the whole see-saw thing. He tried to really second-guess what was happening in the cab, which Sara-Beth had insisted on taking because she was afraid her driver would call her mother in Malibu and tell her where Sara-Beth had gone. But then she had crawled onto his lap and promised never to call him Arno again, and David had pretty much stopped thinking about any playground-equipment metaphors.

"What kind of eggs do you want?" David whispered at her. He was taking breakfast ingredients out of the fridge.

"I don't know," she whispered back. "What kind of eggs do I like?"

When she said this, she sat up straight as though she were awaiting direction.

"Um, I don't know, what kind did your mom make you when you were a kid?"

"Please don't bring her up," she said darkly. "That's not what I mean, anyway. What kind of eggs does SBB like, do you think?"

"Uh," David said. He almost said poached, but then he realized he didn't know how to poach an egg. "Scrambled?" he said eventually.

She nodded, like she was considering the deeper implications of scrambled eggs. "Yes, that's exactly right. Scrambled, with a side of Northern fruit."

David took out a pan and was poised to put it on the stove when he heard a footstep in the hall. He froze, pan in the air like he might smack an intruder with it. Sara-Beth, thankfully, did not freeze. She jumped up and leaned against his back, her silhouette entirely engulfed by his to the person stepping through the kitchen door.

"David," said Sam Grobart. His hair was sticking straight up and he was wearing boxers and his *Psycho-analysts Do It Better* T-shirt. David realized with relief that he was not wearing his glasses. "What are you doing here?"

"Just making a little snack, Dad."

"No, what are you doing back home from Vassar?"

"Uh . . . I came back early to, um, study."

"Good boy. Well, get some rest."

David could feel Sara-Beth's hands running up and down his spine, and he was really hoping that his dad would go away soon.

"That's what I'm going to do at any rate," he said, turning. But before he disappeared back down the hall, something occurred to him. "By the way, David, how did that interview go?"

"Super, Dad," David said, even as the one person who knew that it had not gone super was blowing on his neck. Or, more in the direction of his neck, as the top of her head was at about his chest level. "Almost perfect, I'd say."

As it turned out, a weekend away did just the trick. When I got back to the city I was feeling all amped—everything just seemed possible, you know what I mean? It was nice to know that there was a light at the end of the dark tunnel that was high school, and it was called college.

Seeing my brother had been even better than I'd imagined. He hadn't really made me feel better about myself—at least not in the way I'd been expecting—but he'd taught me an important lesson, which is that when you get a little distance from yourself you really can transform. All these icky feelings about being a shallow person who cared too much about that whole HPSB thing didn't really matter, because by the time I got to college I was going to be known as someone who really cared. About something.

I just hadn't quite figured out what, yet. That was

the one little anxiety I brought back from Vassar with me.

Just to get my foot in the door with this whole caring thing, I attended all my classes on Monday. This seemed to go pretty well. We were reading *Romeo and Juliet* for our Drama as Literature class, and after we all went around reading different parts from a couple scenes in act II, Arno raised his hand.

"I think I finally get what this is all about," Arno said. "I think what Shakespeare is trying to say is that absence is the single most important ingredient to desire."

We had a sub that day—he graduated from Princeton like last year or something so he's really young, and he just teaches part-time. He looked at Arno in this way that made me think he'd never heard the word desire said out loud before.

"Mr. Preston?" I said, raising my hand. "I just wanted to say that I couldn't agree more. Arno, that was a really intelligent point."

And you're thinking right now: he's either being sarcastic or very Dr. Phil, but you would be wrong. I raised my hand because I thought that what Arno said was really smart, and I *cared* enough to say so.

After class we went to the computer lab to check our e-mail. This always makes me a little sad, because Flan always used to send me little stories from her day—even before we were going out, when she was just Patch's little sister to me—and she doesn't anymore. Now, sometimes all that's in my inbox is a mass e-mail about a sample sale or something. Flan would definitely know of some way to practice caring, even if it was just the nearest street corner where some kids were trying to find homes for a new litter of puppies.

There was no platonic love note from Flan this time, although there was a forward from Beatrice, this girl from our Drama as Literature class. It was about a benefit that night for this small, experimental theater company called the Sweet Mercy Theater Company that she'd been ushering for. I skimmed the e-mail and immediately perked up. I knew it wasn't really *that* do-gooderish. I mean it was a party—and I'm not really a theater person—but the party was on Ludlow Street, which usually signals it's the kind of party I'd be down for. And even better, it was a start on the caring thing.

"Hey Arno." I peeked over Arno's shoulder and saw that he was examining the Sarah Lawrence Web site.

"Uh-huh?"

"What are you doing tonight?"

Arno made an indifferent grunting noise and continued scrolling through the pictures in the "campus life" section.

"Do you want to go to a par— a *benefit* with me tonight? It's on Ludlow Street."

"Whatever."

And just like that, we had Monday night plans that were very not us.

was that patch flood waiting on a call?

The cell was going off, and this time it was not the usual annoying jingle. It was the tune of the Beach Boys' "California Girls," which meant that it was Greta calling. Patch knew the phone was in his room because he could hear it. He just didn't know what part of the room. But he was determined to find it before the call went to voicemail.

Patch reached into the pile of semi-dirty clothes on the left side of his bed and started throwing shirts and belts over his head. But the noise remained just as muffled as before and it was not until he was down on his hands and knees that he saw it, underneath the bed. He came up with the phone flipped open.

"Hello?" he heard Greta saying. "Are you there, hello?"

"Hey, Red," Patch said, relieved, leaning back against the bed. He had just gotten back from school, and he was wearing his standard white T-shirt and khakis rolled at the ankle. "I'm here," he added, kicking off the low-top converse he had been wearing without socks.

"What *happened* to you?" she asked. "I kept calling you all weekend."

"I know, that sucked. I couldn't get through to you, either. And the one message from you that I got was all garbled."

"Yeah, I was worried that might happen."

"So did you have a good time?"

"Oh my god, such a good time. I wish you had been there. All of these kids who I was friends with when I was a freshman and they were seniors were there—I think you would really like them—and we all went out on the party circuit. It was hella fun. I mean, I live pretty much without parental constraints, but those college kids—they're something else."

"So, was your . . . ex-boyfriend one of these people?" Patch said, letting his head fall back on the bed. He stared at the glow-in-the-dark stars that Flan had put on the ceiling years ago, as a surprise for his thirteenth birthday. They looked sort of lonely and old during the day.

"Yeah . . . it wasn't a big deal. I mean, it was sort of. It's just that . . . I was going out with him when I was a lot younger and easier to manipulate, you know? So seeing him again—it just made me feel all vulnerable all over again. But whatever. He was nice, and those people are all my friends, so it was never really uncomfortable."

"That's good, I guess."

"Yeah," Greta said, letting out an exaggerated breath of air. "So how was Vassar?"

Patch pushed himself off the floor, and started walking around and gently kicking things on the floor. "The campus was cool I guess, really woodsy. I think I'm going to like that about college."

"Mmm . . ." Greta said, like she was listening more to the sound of his voice than to what he was saying.

"Mickey showed the restaurant pictures to a crowd of hundreds—big success. So it looks like you're going to be a star now, too."

"Oh yeah? That's funny," Greta said, but she sounded kind of distant. The night Mickey took those pictures had been so loose and fun, and everyone had wondered who Patch's beautiful, affectionate, redheaded date was. To Patch, that night seemed far away now. And weirdly, that made him think about how she was a lot closer to, like, a lot of other people . . . guys . . . maybe even that one other guy.

"Greta?" Patch asked, leaning his lean frame against the wall and closing his eyes. "You love where you come from, huh?"

"Yes."

"If we're really going to go to school together, I have to check out some schools out West, huh?"

"Yes."

"Okay, then."

"Sure, it's funny, but I just really like Gatorade . . . ," Mickey said to Lena, Professor Soto's assistant, who was calling from the Sarah Lawrence Art Department. He was in the middle of enumerating his standard on-site lecture demands, and trying hard not to forget anything cool. "So, yeah, I'm going to need like four twenty-ounce bottles wherever I'm staying. Preferably Cool Blue or Glacier Freeze. Also—the last lecture I gave they put me up in the President's Guest Cottage. Do you have one of those?"

"Um, no but . . . ," Lena said haltingly. Mickey listened as she made a counteroffer, and extended his legs so they rested on the large wrought-iron desk in his room.

"Okay, that's fine. Have the limo pick me up on Friday afternoon. I need to keep the departure time loose, though, so have them get here early and they can wait . . ." Suddenly the line went dead. "What the . . . ," Mickey muttered as he put the receiver down and swung his legs off his desk.

He made it to the hall just in time to see his father's fearsome back turning the corner out of view. Ricardo Pardo was built more or less like him—broad shoulders and short, powerful legs that were made for running. And escaping.

Down by his feet, Mickey saw the end of the phone cord. It had been ripped out of the wall. There wasn't much point in wondering who had done the ripping anymore, so Mickey sat down to carefully fuse the brightly colored wires back together. He was crouched over, trying hard not to bash his head into the wall or otherwise physically vent his frustrations, when a gentle voice said: "We used to make life-size sculptures of people out of that type of wire for your dad."

Mickey looked up. It was Caselli, the dude who ran his dad's studio. "Too bad you didn't hang him with it."

Caselli tried to smile, even though smiling made him look kind of silly. He was a big guy with a shaved head, and he was wearing white overalls, which was the same thing that the guys in Ricardo's studio always wore. Mickey was familiar with the warmer, fuzzier side of Caselli, but that didn't make it any less silly. "Ricardo just wants what any father wants: He doesn't want his only son to grow old too quickly."

"Man, we're bros, so I wouldn't want to say you were

wrong," Mickey gave a little tug on the wire, "but you're so wrong."

"Move over," Caselli said. He pulled a pair of pliers out of his pants pocket and began to carefully twist the telephone wires back together. "So what do you think the matter is?"

"I think Dad's just totally jelly about my whole new art thing. I mean, that thing the *Times* ran this morning about how I was an artist of rustling feathers? That's what they used to say about *him*. He just can't handle the fact that the torch has been passed."

"Listen, this isn't an easy time for your dad, professionally. People say his best work is behind him, and that's really frustrating. So hearing himself compared to his son, that's not going to feel nice."

"Okay."

"But I'm going to try and make sure he doesn't take any of that out on you."

"Thanks man," Mickey said, relieved that Caselli had his back but still not quite sure that the elder Pardo deserved any sympathy.

"No problem," Caselli said as he fused a few last wires together. They both sat back on their haunches and considered the situation. Before Mickey got very far, the phone rang in his room. He dashed in to get it.

"The Other Pardo speaking," Mickey said.

"Hi, is this Mickey Pardo?" a woman on the end of the line said. After he'd told her it was, she said, "Well, my name is Pia, from Deitch Projects, and we're having an opening tonight and we would just love it if you made an appearance."

Mickey sat down in his rolling desk chair and pushed off the wall so that he went skidding across the floor. "What's the scene going to be like?" he asked, even though he knew from experience that Deitch Projects was always edgy and cool.

"It's preformancey, and it's going to be very downtown. A little glitter, some electronica. Cass—Cassidy Reed, the performance artist—has even hired pole dancers. We're expecting a number of bold face names, although I'm sure you'll be the one everyone will be dying to meet. Can I put you on the list?"

"I think so," Mickey said, trying to sound very neutral because Caselli was standing right there in the doorway, still checking in.

"It's amazing how . . . theatrical these people look," Jonathan said as he took a sip of his vodka cran.

"Yeah," Arno said, even though he thought they all looked pretty bland. Since Saturday night, he had been consumed by the thought of Lara and what it would be like to attend lectures about truth and beauty with her on leafy afternoons. Nothing else seemed remotely interesting. "I guess that's why they're into theater."

"*That's* brilliant."

"What?" Arno looked at Jonathan, who was wearing charcoal-colored slacks and a T-shirt with a big Red Cross emblem on the chest. He remembered Jonathan buying the shirt at Barneys almost a year ago.

"Never mind," Jonathan said. "Good point. Of course theater people would look theatrical, or of course people who are theatrical dressers would go into theater. That's an excellent point."

"Thanks."

"Christ, I don't know what to do with my hands here. Do you want another drink?"

"Okay." Arno watched as Jonathan made his way through a crowd of cackling, dramatically enunciating people, most of whom were wearing something glittery or shiny. The bar they were in was kind of loud, too. It had fish-shaped Christmas lights strung everywhere, and fishnets hanging from the ceiling. Arno was wearing a black turtleneck sweater and some old Diesels he'd had forever. He hadn't even used product in his hair. The whole look was definitely understated, and the very thought of that word made him feel mature.

He saw Jonathan reach the bar—that was when he felt the gentle bump of skin against his arm and caught a whiff of the distinctive smell of Bubblicious watermelon flavor.

"Wherefore out thou?"

"Excuse me?" Arno looked down to see a petite blonde with great streams of Sarah Jessica Parker hair, staring up at him. Her eyes flashed. Arno had heard of flashing eyes before, but he realized now for the first time what flashing eyes really looked like. Then she blew a big, watermelony bubble.

"You look familiar, and I thought maybe it was because I'd seen you play Romeo before," the girl said. She was wearing a red-and-white checked piece of clothing, which seemed to be both sleeveless top and short-shorts in one, and Arno was pretty sure she had blush on her cheekbones. He hadn't seen a girl wear blush since his fifth grade "Guys and Dolls" play.

"Why would you assume that?"

"Oh, well, you have a kind of lovesick air to you."

"Oh?"

"And you're blandly handsome in that way *all* actors who play Romeo are."

"Oh." Arno's good looks had *never* been called bland before. "That's not where your know me from," he said. "I'm not an actor."

"Really? Because you look super familiar."

"That doesn't surprise me."

"But you're not an actor?" She asked, her eyebrows growing dramatically closer. Arno shook his head. "Then I'm sure I don't know you. My world's pretty small like that."

Arno nodded slowly, enjoying the fact that she knew nothing about the Hottest Private School Boy fiasco. The girl with SJP hair snapped another bubble back into her mouth. "You sure you don't recognize me from someplace else?"

"Nope. But it's nice to meet you now," she said. "I'm Gabrielle. But everyone who knows me calls me Gabby."

"I'm Arno," he said, carefully monitoring her face for any signs of recognition. There were none. "Arno Wildenburger."

"Wow, that's a mouthful," she said. Arno felt more relaxed than he had in weeks. She definitely didn't know him.

"So, you're an actress?"

"Hell no!" This girl wasn't a total beauty, but Arno kind of liked what she could do with her features. He had been thinking about what Lara said—that you didn't really grow up until you'd been in love—and then this girl showed up. It seemed almost *too* convenient, but she was cute, after all. Also, the jumper thing really showed off her legs. She had nice legs.

"But this is your scene?"

"Yeah, I'm a costume designer," she threw up her hands, "I make gowns. This theater company was started by my parents, too. I guess I should cop to that right now. Nepotism—woohoo!"

"Wow, your parents live on the L.E.S.?"

"No, thank god. Not any more. They have a house in Nyack, where they live most of the time, you know, dictating from afar."

"And where do you live?"

"Down the street, around the corner, on Clinton. My parents rented the place for what was a small fortune in

135

1982, but the rent's locked in, so it costs them peanuts now. That's my dowry, apparently." She gave him an audaciously flirty smile. "But enough about me. What's your story?"

"You really don't know?" He still couldn't quite believe that.

"No, why would I? Are you the son of a studio head or something?"

"No. I'm a junior at Gissing."

"Adele Biggs, sophomore," she laughed, putting her hand on her chest. "Wow, you really know how to talk to a girl."

Arno knew this meant that she wasn't impressed by his conversation, but it didn't really bother him. *He* knew that he had had really meaningful conversations with an incredibly sophisticated Sarah Lawrence sophomore just two nights ago. And this Gabby chick *didn't* know that she had just been cast as the girl who would make a grownup out of Arno Wildenburger. There were levels here. He was feeling deeper with every passing moment.

Arno put his arms around her waist, pulled her into him, and kissed her like a leading man. She tasted like watermelon, too, and she smelled a little like sweat and rose perfume, like she had been dancing earlier in the night to Gwen Stefani with her girlfriends.

Everyone made ooh, ah noises, because there was a trapeze artist swinging from the ceiling, but Arno didn't bother to look up.

He didn't let go until he heard a familiar voice, saying: "Excuse me people, but this is a benefit." Arno turned to look at Jonathan, whose eyebrows were raised in disbelief.

"Gabby, this is my friend Jonathan," Arno said. Gabby smiled and looked up at Arno like she was enamored already, so she missed Jonathan mouthing *What about Lara?*

"Jonathan," Arno said, "this is Gabby. I think I'm in love with her."

David had extra-large feet, but he was doing his best to keep them from making a sound as he moved down the hall past the living room. His parents were in there, and luckily for him, they were having a loud conversation about one of his dad's patients. David, still sweaty from his off-season basketball clinic, moved slowly away from them toward his bedroom, where he stealthily turned the knob of the door. Once inside, he turned the lock.

"Hey there," he whispered.

Sara-Beth peeked out from under the covers. "Where have you been, where have you been, where have you *been*?" she blurted out loudly. She was wearing a vintage black slip and her hair was falling messily around her shoulders.

"Shh . . . ," David said, coming over and putting his large, basketball-palming hands on her narrow shoulders. "I'm here now. I just had to go to practice."

"I was so *lonely* . . ."

"I know. I'm sorry. But if I didn't go it would look weird, you know?"

David realized that he was probably more concerned with things looking weird than Sara-Beth, but he was worried that if his parents found out she had been hiding in his bedroom for the past two days things would get really bizarre. He was sure his mother would be upset—he could practically hear her lecture on "boundaries" already—and he really thought that Sara-Beth was too fragile to be sent back home right then. He was also worried that once she met his weirdo parents, SBB wouldn't even want to stay there anymore.

"And I've been hungry."

"I'm really sorry. Can I get you something, maybe?"

"I was so hungry I'm not even hungry anymore. So just don't worry about me, okay?"

"Oh, come on," David said, drawing Sara-Beth's body—which had not gone anywhere—closer into him. "Don't be like that."

"Just don't leave me alone again, okay?"

"Okay, I won't," David said. "How about I make some popcorn and we watch TV?"

"No TV."

"Popcorn and movies?"

"Okay, but only popcorn and old movies," she said, looking up at him with her gigantic blues.

"Why?"

"Stop interrogating me!" she wailed as she threw herself into David's lap.

"All right, all right. Old movies. You stay right here while I make the popcorn, okay? And SB?" He smiled at her and put his index finger across his mouth, signaling quiet. She smiled back, winked, and made the same gesture.

While David was waiting for the popcorn to pop, he wondered if SB wasn't going to derail his whole Potterton career. But she was also so small and gorgeous, and she seemed to require his presence so much, that he was also wondering if she just might be worth it.

He was pouring two glasses of organic lemonade when his mother came into the kitchen.

"David," she said.

"Oh, hey, Mom," David said. "How was your day?"

"Exhausting, as per usual. It was client after client, and my energy is all depleted. But they all—they need me, you know? It's a good exhaustion. I'm tired, but I'm right with the universe."

"That's cool."

"So, your father says that you thought your interview went well."

"Uh, yeah . . ."

"He also said that there was a subtext that he couldn't quite read."

"Subtext?" David said. One thing he'd learned from his parents was how answering questions with questions could really deflect attention.

"David, I just hope you feel you can be honest with us. It's a stressful age."

"Yeah, Mom, totally."

"David, why are you having two glasses of lemonade?"

"Two what? Oh. Mom, I'm an athlete. Whatever portions of things normal kids need, I need approximately double that." David picked up one of the glasses and chugged it. "See? But Mom, I'm really tired. I think I'm just gonna eat some popcorn and hit the hay."

"All right David," she said. "But if there's anything you want to tell me, you know where I'll be."

David waited until his mother was back in the living room, and then he grabbed the popcorn from the microwave and the one glass of lemonade and beat it back to his room. As he shut the door behind him he saw that Sara-Beth was sitting cross-legged on the bed with the blanket thrown over her head like a tent.

"I didn't make a sound," she whispered.

"I'm very impressed," David whispered back.

"Get under here," she said. And he did.

When Patch looked down he had a new text message. He figured it was probably from Jonathan, but when he opened it up he saw that it was from his Mom. This was weird—he hadn't known that she knew how to text. Also, she and his dad were in Greenwich that week, and she was usually too busy relaxing when she was at the Flood compound there to call the city.

The message read: *Heyday in town today please order dinner in and get him to talk. FF says hes been in silent period xx mom*

Patch jumped on his skateboard, and as he rode out of Union Square in the direction of home he hit redial.

"Miss me already?" Greta said.

"Always."

"Good. Hey, I was thinking, maybe we could get three pug puppies. Don't you think that would be better? Then, even if one is sleeping, the other will still have a friend."

"Okay," Patch said. "Hey, I've got news. My uncle Heyday is in town."

"Heyday? What kind of name is that?"

"Well, you've noticed that my name is Patch and my older sister's name is February. It's a Flood kind of name, I guess."

"Hmm, yeah, now that you mention it . . ."

"He's just spent six months in the Mojave by himself." Patch came off Fourteenth Street and went flying down Eighth Avenue.

"Oh, *that* uncle Heyday. Is this the same uncle who sailed around the Indian ocean on a homemade raft?"

"Yup. But he's done a lot of time in your home state, so I thought he might have some good ideas about, you know . . ."

"Oh awesome. Does he know about me yet?"

"No, but he will soon," Patch said as he turned on to Perry Street. "Call me later?"

"Heart you." Greta said, and he could hear her squinch up her nose as she did.

"Yeah."

Patch ollied onto the curb and coasted to the steps of his family's town house, where he was met by a welcome sight.

"So this is what civilization looks like," Heyday Flood boomed from his perch at the top step. He looked like an older Patch, with his tanned face and overgrown hair, except a little more leathery from his extra twenty-five years in the sun. He was wearing a white Baja pullover, pink swim trunks, and flip-flops, and he was sipping from one of the Flood's goblet-sized wine glasses. The bottle—clearly from the Flood's basement wine cellar— was sitting next to him.

"Mom said Dad said you weren't speaking," Patch said with a smile.

"Six months in the Mojave, no talking. No people either. I'm still remembering how to do this, so forgive me if the volume's a little high."

Heyday stood and embraced Patch, and then poured his nephew a glass of wine. "It's good to see you, dude," Patch said.

"Likewise. Man, you don't know what a town house and a glass of Malbec mean until you've spent six months dodging the heat of day and cold of night." Heyday took a reflective sip and continued in an even louder voice. "As T. E. Lawrence put it, 'By day, the hot sun fermented us; and we were dizzied by the beating wind. At night we were stained by dew, and shamed into pettiness by the innumerable silences of stars.'"

"That sounds intense."

"Eh, kind of. Keeps you young. Reminds you who you are." He did a quick back-cracking stretch move and appraised two Manolo-clad women clicking down Perry Street in the direction of new bars. "Man, there are some pretty women in this city."

Two generations of Flood men meditated on this for a moment, and then Patch said, "So what do you do now?"

"Well, that's a big question mark, isn't it? But before the Mojave, I was doing forest firefighting. It's a dangerous hobby, and I had to move myself away from that, quiet the mind a little bit—but it's also of huge importance. In some cases, you're saving trees that are older than baseball." Heyday took a sip of his wine. "But there are other vocations, too."

"Like what?" Patch loved his uncle. He was maybe the only guy in the world that made Patch look focused, not that Patch usually thought about such things.

"Oh, there's fishing in Alaska, for instance. There's a direct hit to the soul. Grape picking. I don't know if you know this about me, but I'm also a licensed nurse, and that might call me again."

"Nursing?"

"Patch, we Floods are highly blessed. The family's system of trusts has allowed me to circle the globe I don't know how many times and break bread with *beau coup de* kinds of people. But we are all born to serve. We must all shape ourselves with work."

"Huh. I guess this is going to sound really dumb, but I never thought about it that way . . ."

"Not dumb at all," Heyday drained the last of the wine from his glass and then found that the bottle was empty, too. "Hey, kiddo, why don't you go see about another bottle. And then, like it or not, we're going to talk about you."

A bottle and a half later, with the sun going down over Perry Street, Heyday rested an arm around Patch's shoulder and said, "So your mother says you've been doh-mess-dah-cated."

"I don't know about all that."

"Tell your uncle, kiddo."

"Her name's Greta—she's beautiful and adventurous and she doesn't mind ruining her shoes." Patch tried to think of the perfect way to describe Greta, but the right words escaped him. "She's just natural, you know?"

"There's a catch, I can hear it in your voice."

"Well, we have this whole idea about going to college together."

"Sounds great."

"But the thing is, she wants to go to a West Coast school, and I want to go East Coast."

"Why do you want to do that?"

"I don't know, because a landscape of strip malls doesn't interest me?" Patch sighed. "I guess it actually is important to be on the same coast as my friends. I may not seem like the most clique-oriented dude, but it's important that they be near me, you know?"

"Well, I suggest you check out some places in California, anyway."

"I know I should. And I will."

"It will make your lady happy," Heyday said. He took a breath. "And while you're at it, you should check out my alma mater."

"You went to college?" Patch chuckled. "I have a hard time picturing that."

"Well, it's not your usual lecture-hall-by-day, puke-on-the-lawn-by-night experience. It's near Mammoth, where your father and I took you skiing as a young dude, and it's also a ranch. Unlike most schools, an appreciation of labor is combined with intellectual pursuits—many of my mornings there began at six a.m., milking the cows and whatnot."

"Man, that sounds just right for Greta and me," Patch said with relief. He knew Heyday's visits always came with good advice, and he could hardly wait to call Greta and tell her. "What's this place called?"

"It's called Deep Springs, kiddo, and I think it might be your spiritual home." Heyday paused to drink the last of the wine from the bottle. "But it would be impossible for you to attend with your girlfriend, I'm afraid. It is, by Deed of Trust, a dudes only school."

Patch turned away from Heyday, and looked down Perry Street toward the water. He couldn't look at his freewheeling uncle right then, because for the first time in his life, Patch Flood felt trapped.

i find out how dark it is when you care

I was really beginning to see how the world works
sometimes, and after I watched Arno use our theater benefit as a way to pick up one girl so that he
could fall in love with another (if I thought about this
too hard, I would be thinking cynically, so I'm just
not going to do it), I went home and folded up all the
clothes I didn't wear anymore and put them in
Garden of Eden bags to send down to the Salvation
Army. Or up to the Salvation Army—wherever it is.

I called my mom to ask her, because I knew
she's done that before. But she was about to be
seated at Da Silvano, where she was having dinner
with her business manager, so she said she was
going to have to call me back.

In the meantime, I went for a walk outside. It was
twilight, and there were people selling fake hand-
bags in the streets. I walked all the way down to
Houston, where the traffic was stalled in both
directions, and then I walked back up toward my

apartment. On the way, though, I passed through NYU territory. That was when I started spotting all these flyers for different collegey activities. None of them sounded all that altruistic, but they triggered my memory.

You know how I mentioned my stepbrother, Rob? Well, when he threw this big, illegal party a bunch of weeks ago that was supposedly to celebrate Arno but was actually just a big money-making scheme, he did this crazy lame thing. He went around tearing down a bunch of flyers for this do-gooder event that was happening on the same night so that there would be no competition for his party.

Anyway, all these flyers around Washington Square Park reminded me of Lily Maynard at Barton Day and all her altruistic event-throwing. She had really, really cared about that night, whatever it was, and had been devastated about Rob's Machiavellian poster doings. So I looked through the phonebook on my cell and eventually, when I got down to the Ms, I found that she had somehow managed to get in there. Maynard, Lily, a 212 number. Of course Lily Maynard wouldn't have a cell phone. Cell phones were only useful to people who were concerned about their evening plans. I wasn't even sure why I had one anymore.

But as long as I still had a cell I could call Lily Maynard and ask her for some advice. As I walked out of the park, I listened to her home phone ring once, twice, three times. I was sort of relieved— this was one call that was going to voicemail. After all, I hadn't thought at all about how I was going to begin this conversation. I was listening to the sixth ring fade away when the phone picked up and a girl said, "Barton Day Homeless Outreach HQ."

I paused. "Are you at school?"

"This is Barton Day Homeless Outreach. Do you need shelter tonight?"

"Um, I'm not homeless. I just wanted to talk to Lily."

There was a prolonged silence, and then: "This is she."

"Lily, this is Jonathan. From Gissing."

"Oh, hey Jonathan. What's going on?"

"You are at school, aren't you?"

"Yes. I mean, who else is going to staff Homeless Outreach HQ on their off time?"

"Wow, that's really nice of you. I mean, you must really care."

"Well, yeah, I do. But I also get a lot of homework done on nights like these."

"Oh."

"So what's up?"

"Well, see," I filled my cheeks up with air and then let them out slowly, wondering how I was ever going to explain this. Lily Maynard is one of those soft-faced, shiny-haired people who have already rewritten their college essay about how they plan to end hunger in Africa by age twenty-five, three times. She got really excited about helping people, and she meant it. Why would a person like that take my plight seriously? "I went up to Vassar last weekend, you know, to see my older brother Ted, and—"

"No way, no way, no way!" Lily squealed.

"No, I did," I said slowly, wondering why Lily sounded so excited. Was it that unbelievable that I would go up there to visit Ted? "I mean, I went up there to have fun, too, but also to see my brother."

"Yes . . . go on. Please."

"Anyway, I just started feeling kind of bad about my relatively low level of social engagedness. And I wanted to start doing stuff. That shows the world I care."

"Oh," Lily said, and then paused like she was sorting something out about me. "I see. That's . . . that's great, Jonathan."

"Are you mad at me?" I blurted out without thinking. She sounded kind of mad.

"No," Lily said slowly. "No, not *mad* at all. Can I ask you something? Did you know your brother used to be the president of Homeless Outreach in New York private schools?"

"Man, I guess I didn't."

"Yeah, well, he was. Can I tell you something? I mean, we're friends right?"

"Um, yeah. And yeah," I added quickly, "we're friends."

"I've always had the *biggest* crush on your brother."

"Oh."

"The only reason I could imagine you were calling was to tell me you had a message from him. . . . That's why I got all excited."

"No. No, I wasn't. He, uh, has a girlfriend at Vassar."

"Can you hold on one second?" I heard Lily moving around in the background, blowing her nose. I was pretty sure she wasn't crying though— Lily was always blowing her nose. When she came back she said, "Forget I said that, okay?"

"You got it. Maybe we can make a deal, and you won't tell anybody what I said?"

"Oh, no no no. Jonathan, I'm sorry I derailed all of your good intentions with my selfish feelings."

"It's really okay."

"No, it's not. And I'm going to make it up to you. Can you get out of school on Friday?"

"That's never really been a problem for me."

"Great, my friend Ava just got involved with this urban gardening program that's creating a community garden on an empty lot on the West Side. Every Friday they're having 'work parties' to get it set up and running. It will be a great opportunity for you to volunteer, and show that you care about neighborhoods and the environment. Ava says they're really fun, and . . ." Lily paused self-consciously, and I could tell that she was still embarrassed about the whole Ted thing. "Well, let's just say that Ava knows a lot more about fun than I do."

I told her I was sure that wasn't true, and asked her to give me the address. As she did I wrote it down. This program did sound really cool, although something about the whole idea left me feeling unsettled.

"Hey, Jonathan? If Ted ever mentions me . . ."

"You'll be the first to know," I said, waving at the doorman and heading for the elevator. "And thanks, Lily."

mickey runs into an old special someone

Mickey commandeered a plate of canapés from a passing waiter and surveyed his third art opening of the evening. The two models he started hanging out with at Deitch Projects the night before, and who had been with him since then, were being interviewed by a Page Six reporter and were posing for pictures with any quasi-celebrity who walked by. Mickey—who was wearing a wife beater and red-and-black striped drawstring pants—was trying to hang back.

The art opening was for an old painter friend of Ricardo, and Mickey knew that if someone asked for his opinion he was going to have to admit that he thought the show sucked. He might also tell them that he thought this party was too freaking stuffy.

His opinion had been asked several times the night before, and every unflattering thing he'd said had been recorded by one or more of the tabloids. (*Newsday*: "Famous Sculptor's Son Bites Hand that Feeds Him.") Mickey might have missed this fact, except that his dad had clipped them all and taped them to his door along with a two-page letter in Spanish explaining his failures as a son.

Mickey had decided that getting lots of un-Ricardo-related coverage would be the sweetest revenge. So he watched happily as the models told the Page Six person all kinds of outrageous Mickey anecdotes. And now he had his own plate of canapés to boot.

"What are you doing here?" said a sweet and familiar voice close by.

"Phil!" Mickey managed, as he sucked the last of a canapé into his mouth and down his throat. He tried to keep from choking as he took in the sight of his ex-girlfriend in a fitted camo jacket and black miniskirt. "What are *you* doing here?"

"My new girlfriend's an art critic for the Barnard paper," Philippa said. She smiled and squeezed Mickey's hand. "That's her over there. God I'm glad to see you here."

Mickey looked, and saw a tall girl with her short hair parted at the side and slicked back so that it tucked behind her ears. She was wearing fitted black slacks and a white button-down shirt with a big, stiff collar, and she was talking animatedly with the artist. "Yuh," said Mickey, "she looks like the girlfriend-stealing type."

"No joking like that!" Philippa said. "I really like this one."

"Okay. What's her name?"

"Stella. I met her at the Hungarian Pastry shop on Amsterdam Avenue. She was studying for this class called The Male Gaze in American Cinema, and I was having a croissant before school."

Mickey looked back at the girlfriend. She had lit a cigarette, and one eye appeared to be twitching as she talked. "Man, it's good to see you."

"Likewise. We should practice being friends more."

"Totally." Mickey thought to offer Philippa a canapé, but she waved it away. He discretely put the plate on the floor behind him. "So what's new?"

"Not much. Looking forward to summer. Hanging out with Stella. My parents are insisting I go to Maine with them for a *month*, though, which is going to be such a drag."

"Mmm, yeah." Mickey's eye wandered to the models, who were laughing loud and horselike now.

"So what's up with the models, Mickey?"

"I don't know, I think posing for pictures is, like, their job," Mickey said defensively. Why was Philippa chastising him? It wasn't like he had sought the models out. "Your new girlfriend has a twitch, by the way."

"She does not! That just happens sometimes, when

she's, like, having an idea." There was an awkward silence, and then he saw Stella the Barnard art critic approaching them.

"What's up babe," she said, putting both arms around Philippa from behind.

"Hey, I'm . . . ," Mickey started.

"The ex?" she cut him off sharply. "I guessed as much."

"Well, it sucks to meet you, too."

Stella laughed like that was the funniest thing in the world. She didn't seem to take it personally at all. "Good one. So, are you a one-hit wonder, Mr. Pardo, or have you got the stuff?"

"Well, I'm probably too biased to answer that question. But I believe my second lecture, this Saturday night at lovely Sarah Lawrence college, will answer that question."

"Very impressive," Stella smiled. "I look forward to hearing how it goes. Anyway, don't you think these paintings suck?"

"I find them a little dull, yes," Mickey said cautiously.

"I mean, hasn't the time for large-scale self-portraits in shades of tropical rainforest come and gone?"

Mickey snickered.

"Oh, come on guys," Philippa said. She paused, seeming to realize that a plea for niceness was not going to fly here. "Doesn't everyone come for free wine anyway?"

They all laughed loudly at that. Several people turned to look at them curiously, and then the two models did, too. They narrowed their eyes at Stella and Philippa, but they didn't come back—apparently they knew that they had been replaced.

"Oh, there's the Village Voice critic," Stella said. "I'm going to go have a word. Nice to meet you, Pardo Dos."

Mickey saluted her, and watched her saunter over to a balding man with a shoulder-length fringe of hair and wire-rim glasses.

"Stella's so smart it's intimidating sometimes," Philippa said with a sigh.

"Oh, whatever," Mickey said. "She's not *that* smart. I should know. I just lectured at Vassar."

Philippa shook her head doubtfully. "Be careful with that absurd confidence. It could get you in big trouble," she said, taking his hand affectionately. "I should go over there. She'll want to introduce me. But it's really good to see you. Let's get together soon, okay?"

Mickey nodded, and watched her approach Stella and the Village Voice guy shyly. She turned back and gave him a little wave with the tips of her fingers, and all of a sudden Mickey couldn't help but think that maybe, just maybe, this whole lesbian thing was going to blow over . . . and soon.

arno would just like to know
what meaningful really means

Arno was sitting on the grand stone steps in front of Gissing, getting more and more irritated by the Sarah Lawrence directory assistance.

"Well, I don't know her last name. Can't you just do a search for Lara?" He was wearing white cords, a faded I-heart-New-York T-shirt, and flip-flops, which he realized was not an outfit that implied he was going to spend all day in class. "I mean, she's from Napa, does that help? How many Laras from Napa wineries do you have there?" He brushed his bangs away from his eyes and waved at Mrs. Lambers, his bio teacher, who was trudging up the steps with a great pile of graded tests. "Okay, fine. Fine. How about . . . hold on. I have a call waiting. Can you hold on?" he clicked over. "Wild-enburger."

"Hi *Wildenburger.*"

"Gabby?" Arno said, flashbacking to two nights ago. He had been so busy trying to contact Lara to tell her he'd already been in love that he had forgotten about the said object of his affection. "How did you get this number?"

"Um, well, there was a pen. And a piece of paper. And you used the pen to write on the paper, 'Gabby, call me sometime, xx Arno.' But that's the abridged version. All of this was after you said you were in love with me. I still haven't figured out whether that was just the booze talking or what."

"Hey, I'm about to be late for school. What's up?"

"School? Going back to school after lunch on Wednesdays is like so 2005."

"Oh, really. What are you doing?"

"Well, I'm really very concerned about my tan. Also, my skeeball game is really suffering because of my late hours at the sewing machine. So what do *you* think I'm going to do?"

"Um . . . I don't know, I'm really not good at guessing games."

Gabby made an exaggerated exasperation sound. "Well, going to Coney Island, of course."

"Oh."

"Well, aren't you a chatty Kathy today. Are you coming with me or not?"

Arno looked down at his feet. He *was* already wearing flip-flops. "Okay."

Two hours later, he and Gabby were walking hand in hand down the boardwalk. She was wearing a turquoise halter bikini top and big espresso-colored sarong-style pants that sat low on her hips and showed off the jutting bones there. She was also wearing several heavy gold chains. They were the perfect picture of hipster-couple-does-rundown-resort town.

"Don't you just love it here?" Gabby said, throwing her arms up and breathing in the sea air.

"It's a little dirty, don't you think?"

"Oh, it's camp. All of it's delicious camp. Speaking of delicious, I think they have Smirnoff Ice there. Will you go get us some?"

Arno did what she asked, but he was feeling sort of silly. He was enjoying Gabby and everything, but did they really have to drink beer that tasted like juice? It didn't seem very meaningful. They continued down the beach, drinking their Smirnoff Ice from big Styrofoam cups.

Gabby took a reflective sip. "So, I can't figure it out."

"What?"

"Whether I like you or not. I mean, you're good-looking."

"Thanks."

"Mostly in an actor way, but you do have sort of an

edge. But you never say much. So what I'm wondering is, are you mysterious . . . or stupid?"

"Huh."

"Today I'm leaning toward mysterious. I think you have a secret, Arno Wildenburger."

"Oh?" Arno felt a nice, warm feeling spreading through his chest. "You're pretty insightful. For your age."

"That had better be a joke. Cuz if it's not, then I really will know that you're stupid."

"It was a joke."

She swung in front of him and gave him a wide, toothy smile. Arno pulled her up to him and kissed her. She did taste good. They kept kissing, until a bunch of guys started yelling at them to get a room. Gabby pulled away, and gave the guys a disgusted look. Then she was distracted by something else.

"Look! Skeeball! C'mon, let's play skeeball. Can we pretty please play skeeball?" Gabby was jumping up and down and pointing at a row of amusement park–style games.

"Okay," Arno said. He took some quarters from his pocket and handed two of them over to Gabby. She stuffed her quarters in the machine and the balls plunked down.

"Come on, champ," she said. She pulled her arm

back, paused for effect, and then let the ball go skidding up the plank and into the 300 bucket. She jumped up and down again, which annoyed Arno for reasons he wasn't entirely sure of.

"Nice shot," he said, although he didn't really mean it. He tossed a ball up the ramp, and it hit the rim of the hundred bucket and fell away, pointless.

"Lordie, did you learn skeeball from a girl?" Gabby twisted her hair back, and let fly another 300 pointer. "Scooooooore!" she cried jumping up and down.

Arno managed 200 points on his next try, but with one ball left, it wasn't looking good for him. Gabby took her last ball, blew on it, did a little dance, and prepared for the throw. She stretched her arm back and then let it fly—a perfect shot up the center of the lane. The ball hit the divider between the 400 and 500 buckets, teetered, and then fell in for 500 points. As soon she started doing her dance, Arno leaned forward and tossed his last ball, softball style, into the 1,000 point bucket. The flashing lights on top of the machine went wild, and the tickets starting pouring out.

Gabby stopped leaping around and singing "I win, I win." She looked up at him, seeming a little stunned. "What a fluke that was," she said.

"Maybe I was just psyching you out my first two

turns. I should warn you, one of my many secrets is that I'm a shark."

"Oh, whatever."

"C'mon," Arno said, collecting his tickets. "I'll buy you a teddy bear."

"I don't want your teddy bear," Gabby said, narrowing her eyes. "You cheated. I don't know how, but you must have." She crossed her arms over her chest and stomped over to the railing of the boardwalk.

Arno couldn't believe this. Fighting over skeeball was possibly the lowest he'd ever sunk. But if he left now, he wasn't sure if he could technically still say he had already been in love, so he went over to the booth at the end of the row of skeeball machines and handed over his tickets.

"Does this get me the pink panther?"

"No," said the heavy-set stuffed animal vendor, "and I saw what you did."

"Oh, come on," Arno said. "Everyone cheats at skeeball. And the other animals suck. Can I please have the pink panther?"

"Maybe I would if . . . but you're a cheater, so I don't see why I should help you out."

Arno looked down at his chest and remembered the rush he'd felt with Lara. Now, looking down in the general vicinity of his heart, he didn't know what he saw there.

"Oh, for fuck's sake," Arno said, a little more gruffly then he had meant to. He put a twenty down on the counter and stared at the guy until he lifted one of the big pink panthers down from the display and handed it over. "Thanks man," Arno said crisply, and walked back over to where Gabby was standing, staring out at sea.

"Hey gorgeous, I got you something," he said, handing her the pink panther.

"I love the pink panther," she said, gasping and hugging it to her body. "Thank you. I'm sorry I acted like a baby, but I'm just a really competitive person." She sighed. "And I'm an only child."

"Me too," Arno said.

"Well, I guess it's meant to be, then. Come on!" Gabby said, dragging him by the hand down the board-walk. "Let's go ride the cyclone. Can we ride the cyclone, *please*?"

Arno said yes, but his heart wasn't in it. It was tough going, but if this—and by this, he meant Gabby—was what he had to get through to get a girl like Lara, he was just going to have to take a deep breath and ride the roller coaster. As they walked across the boardwalk toward the rickety-looking structure rising into the blue Coney Island sky, Arno realized that he had missed his therapy session entirely.

david goes home to his lady

It took David a good half hour to convince his Potterton friends that he really wasn't down for an after-school game of pickup basketball. He never managed a very good reason why, but eventually they gave up on him and headed over to the courts at West Fourth Street. As soon as they were gone, David used his long, lean, basketball-playing legs to carry him back to his apartment as fast as humanly possible.

It was a bright day with an epically blue sky, and all the mothers in the Village were out with their strollers. David weaved between them, almost coming to a jog by the time he reached the lobby of his building.

He opened the door and as noiselessly as possible slipped inside and began tip-toeing down the hall. His parents were talking in the living room, so he was concentrating very hard on being quiet when his foot slid on the recently-shined hardwood floor and he went flying backward. He managed to keep from totally wiping out by slamming one hand against the wall and swinging the rest of his body into the wall, too. It was not a quiet move.

David froze, and waited for his parents to appear. He knew this meant another half hour of talking about college and scholarships and community service before he got to rescue Sara-Beth from her loneliness. Weirdly, though, no one seemed to have noticed David's blunder. His parents voices were still chatting away on the other side of the wall.

"The celebrity industrial complex," his dad was saying, "as I call it, can be very harmful to the self. It is, unique among psychiatric complexes, swayed by the opinion of the whole world. Or at least, a big portion of it."

David's dad rarely talked about celebrity, much less the concept of celebrity. This couldn't be good. David cautiously moved along the wall and peered through the open French doors into the living room. And there was a very weird sight. His parents were both pacing the floor, and there was Sara-Beth Benny, wearing her gigantic black sunglasses and the same slip she had been wearing for two days. She was lying on the couch, with her head resting against a cushion and her bare feet sticking up at the end. David could see, even from the doorway, that tears were running down her face.

"Let's talk about dreams," David's mother said.

"Yes, let's," his father said.

"Well, I dreamed last night that I had a sister. And all the kids in school made fun of her, because she was fat and she didn't know how to dress right. But I was too busy being this, like, famous party girl and so I didn't even notice until it was too late, and then she killed herself, and I didn't do anything to protect her!" Sara-Beth wailed.

"That's a very powerful dream," David's mother said. Tears were now flowing, full force, down Sara-Beth's face.

"I agree," his father said.

"What are you *doing*?" David said, stepping into the room.

"David," his mother said.

"Stop it!" he yelled.

"David," his father said.

"You're hurting her," David went on. Sara-Beth lifted her glasses onto her forehead and gave him a look. Her eyes were red and her face was pale with emotion.

Sam Grobart took a step toward his son. "David, I thought you would have had more respect for the process of therapy, growing up the way you did."

"Your new friend is a very wounded girl," Hilary added.

"They're not hurting me," Sara-Beth said. "They

just . . . they just . . . they just know how I like my eggs."

"Scrambled?" David said in a very small voice.

"Yes," his mother said. "Scrambled."

"David?"

David blinked at his father. "Yes, Dad?"

"There's a lot of work to be done. Emotional work." He sucked in his breath. "Now, I think we're going to all have to sit down and talk. A lot of talking. About what this girl has gone through, and how she can start living her best life."

"Are you okay?" David asked Sara-Beth. She sat up on the couch and nodded.

"We've been talking about the first time she realized that she was famous," Hilary said softly.

"Yes, like I said, there's going to be a lot of talking. So what I suggest is we order in Empire Szechuan and eat Grobart-family style. We put an old sheet on the ground and sit cross-legged and we can continue this very productive, this very *necessary*, conversation." Sam Grobart lifted a finger to illustrate his point and then dashed from the room. "I'll get the menu," he called. They could hear him rummaging in the kitchen.

The light of early evening was coming through the window and playing on Sara-Beth's pale skin. She gave David a long, deep stare, like she was helpless and she trusted him to care for her. David almost forgot that his mother was in the same room as them, but then he looked up and saw that she was staring at Sara-Beth in this weird but definitely loving way, too. Then David's dad came back in the room.

"Can we please, please get duck?" Sara-Beth said.

Nobody said anything for a moment, and then Sam barked, "Of course. Of course you can. Honey-glazed Chinese duck? You got it. David, your usual broccoli beef?"

"Yeah, that sounds good."

"Hil, I'm assuming sesame chicken for you? And I'll have the prawns Szechuan. And we can share dishes in whatever way makes us all most comfortable. Mmm, delicious." He dashed from the room again. Then they heard him call, "Hil, where's the bleeping phone?!"

Hilary rolled her eyes. "How should I know?"

"Found it!"

David watched his mom sit down on the couch and begin stroking Sara-Beth's hair. David realized that it would probably be a good time to take his backpack off, so he did. "So you're not mad, Mom?"

"Of course not, honey bunch," she said.

"So, can we keep her? I mean, can she stay?"

Sara-Beth and his mom both looked up at him with deeply sincere expressions on their faces. "I really think that's for the best," his mother said. "Don't you?"

171

After school on Wednesday Patch skateboarded over to the East Side. It was an intensely bright day, and the park had been overtaken by sunbathers and people on rollerblades. The smell of grass and horse manure mingled in the air. When he got to the corner of Sixty-eighth and Park he skidded to a stop, took a navy blazer out of his backpack, and put it on.

He hadn't even known he had a blazer, and had been surprised to find it hidden away in the corner of his closet. It felt entirely wrong on him. But his college advisor had told him the Brown prospective student event he'd been invited to was jackets required, so he put the thing on, waved at the doorman, and rode the gilded elevator to the eighth floor.

"You must be Patch Flood," said the woman who met him at the elevator. She was in her early thirties and even though she was dressed very casually in khaki slacks and a fitted black t-shirt, her hair was done up in a chignon to reveal the two giant, shining diamond studs she wore. "I'm Gillian, Brown alumnus, and I am so glad you could make it. I just wanted to say that I really feel I've come to know you, from all the press, and, well, it's wonderful to meet you in the flesh."

Patch tried to smile at her, but smiling when he didn't mean it was virtually impossible for him. "Thanks," he managed.

"Won't you come into the living room? You have a guest waiting, I believe."

That didn't bode well.

She led him into a huge room with expansive windows and a view down onto the treetops of Central Park. Patch never really got why people liked living uptown, but he always did enjoy seeing the park that way—it looked like a blanket had been thrown over the center of Manhattan, and it made him understand why one might put up with all the lapdogs and jerks in suits. A little bit.

"Would you like some tea?" Gillian asked him.

"Sure," Patch responded, looking around at the other high school students standing around drinking from little porcelain cups. The guys were all in jackets, and the girls were all in neat skirts. More than one of the guys was wearing a Brown T-shirt underneath a blazer. Among them was an older, tall, sun-tanned guy in a frayed corduroy blazer, sticking out like a grandpa at an Ashlee Simpson concert.

"Dude, what are you doing here?" Patch asked, embracing his uncle.

"Came to check out what high school girls look like these days," Heyday said with a chuckle. Then he gave Patch a serious look. "Just kidding, youngin'. Your college advisor called to remind you about the event, and I took the message. Thought you could use some backup with all the stiffs."

Patch surveyed the scene and acknowledged that this was probably true. "Hey man, I hope you're not disappointed that I'm still looking at schools out here," he said. "I mean, Deep Springs sounds great, but I do really want to go to the same school as Greta. And with my friends. That school strikes out in both categories."

Heyday gestured to him that it wasn't a big deal. "Don't trip, kiddo," he said. Then Brock, this guy Patch knew from Turner, and some other guys they went to school with approached the Flood men. There were hand-slapping hellos and a few pats on the back.

"So, I didn't know you were thinking about Brown," Brock said resentfully, as though this news somehow lessened his ability to get in.

"I was," Patch said, still almost wishing he didn't have to say so in front of his uncle. "But my girlfriend is from the West Coast, and Brown is the only school that appeals to her for some reason."

"That girl from Pardo's photos?" one of Brock's friends asked. He was wearing a navy blazer and he had pale skin and greasy hair. Patch was pretty sure that he went to Turner, although there were a bunch of guys who looked like that. It irritated him that this guy could picture Greta naked.

"Yeah, she lives in California," Patch said pointedly.

"Which is where I went to college," Heyday interrupted with a crooked smile.

The guys all looked up at him. Before they could say anything, Gillian reappeared with tea. Patch and Heyday both took their porcelain teacups and saucers, and then the older man leaned toward her and said, "Sweetheart, any chance I could get a little bit of the good stuff in this?" He winked and patted her on the butt. Patch was worried for a second that his uncle had forgotten the rules of society, but Gillian didn't seem to mind. She whispered, "Sure," breathily, and hurried off.

"So where'd you go to school, man?" Brock asked.

"A very small, labor-intensive school called Deep Springs," Heyday said, accepting a shot of scotch in his tea from Gillian, who then lingered behind them listening in. "Chances are you've never heard of it. But it is one of the few institutions that produces *men*, as opposed to, say, employable young people."

"I've heard of that place," the kid who had wanted to know about Greta said.

"Oh?" said Heyday. "We Deep Springers don't want it to get too well known. But it is a remarkable experience."

"Yeah," the kid went on, sneering, "that's the one where it's just guys and you always have to have some farm job to do. After four years of New York private school, I'd like to sleep in a little, you know what I mean?"

"Or get laid in my own bed occasionally," one of the other guys added.

Patch found himself rolling his eyes. "Come on, like you guys don't sleep late with girls in your beds now." He paused and looked at his uncle, who didn't seem offended at all by what these guys were saying. He did seem amused by Patch's irritation. "It's just weird to me that you would want to go to college and keep being the same people you were in high school," Patch said quietly. "College means you get to go to a new city and learn new things. You could make yourself into an entirely different person, but you just want to be the same snide, lazy kids you've always been. That seems so boring to me."

Heyday raised his eyebrows and took a long sip of his tea. He appeared to be holding in a laugh. "Spoken like a true Deep Springs man," he said into his cup.

Before Patch could respond to any of this, his cell phone went off in his pocket. He wasn't sure whether he should be more annoyed by these dumbasses he went to school with or by his uncle for getting him into the conversation in the first place. He pulled the cell out. "Excuse me," he said, and walked over to the window.

"Greta?" he said, when he was far enough away to not be overheard.

"Patch?" Greta said in a very small voice. "Where are you?"

"At the Brown prospie event." It sounded like she had been crying.

"Oh," Greta said. She paused and took a deep breath. "Patch, there's something I did that I have to tell you about . . ."

"Mickey! Mickey! Mickey!"

The paparazzi were straining behind their ropes. Mickey paused for a moment on the impossibly grand steps of the Metropolitan Museum and made a show of waving and blowing kisses to the press. He was trying hard to behave himself, but he was growing irritated by the klieg lights' blaze already. Even though what he really wanted to do was yell, "I'm an artist not your circus monkey!" Mickey air-guitared for the pleasure of his audience and then hurried up the steps while their cheers still lingered in the air.

At the top, a familiar figure was waiting for him.

"You handled that well," said Philippa, who was standing with Stella at the top of the stairs. She reached out and, with a motherly gesture, tamed Mickey's hair.

"Thanks," Mickey said, "I'm so psyched you guys are with me. I think it's going to be a bunch of stiffs in there."

It was the gala opening for some photographer or

other. Mickey wasn't even sure who it was, but he had promised Stella that he'd get them all invited to a big art event, and this seemed sure to be the biggest. Mickey's opinions had taken on a wild currency over the past two days. People seemed to hang on his every word and the invites were multiplying in his e-mail, being hand-delivered to his house, appearing just about everywhere.

"You girls look gorgeous," Mickey said as they passed into the dramatic lobby of the Met. Stella was wearing a tuxedo that, like his own, was somewhat baggy and off, and Philippa was wearing a Diane von Furstenberg wrap dress that he had seen many times before. This touched him, for some reason. She looked beautiful in it.

The lobby was filled with well-dressed grown-ups who were chatting politely in small groups. There was a string quartet hidden somewhere, playing soothing music, and waiters hovered with trays of champagne.

"I could probably do this every night," Philippa said as a waiter stopped by to give them drinks.

"You'd get bored," Stella said dryly. She cocked an eyebrow and surveyed the crowd like she was looking for people she recognized.

"Ah, come on," Mickey said, gulping his champagne. Even though he was growing leery of his role as an art world sideshow, he thought Stella's ennui was kind of lame. "How can you not love a party at the Met? They have pyramids here, for crying out loud."

Stella appeared to be considering whether Mickey's comments constituted a threat. She shrugged her shoulders and said, "You're right. What's to complain about? It's like every bright star in the art world is here."

"Ahem," Mickey cleared his throat.

"Of which you are the brightest," Stella added, smiling with real affection this time.

They wandered through the antiquities collection and into the large glass-ceilinged room that housed the Temple of Dendur. The reflection mirror was dark and mysterious, and art world luminaries lingered around it drinking from champagne flutes and chatting in hushed tones.

"It's beautiful," Philippa said, looking up at the dramatic Egyptian temple, transplanted to one of the Met's gigantic rooms.

"You know that represents a legacy of imperial exploitation," Stella said.

"I know," Philippa said quietly. "I still think it's pretty amazing."

Mickey spotted a reporter approaching them from across the room. Like everyone else there, he was wearing a suit, although his long hair was tucked into his coat. Stella kissed the art guy on both cheeks and threw her head back in laughter.

"Stella already knows the photographer's work pretty well," Philippa said, as she and Mickey drew back from the conversation.

"Oh, right. Well, she's the art critic and everything," Mickey said. "Hey, they look pretty busy. You want to check out the buffet?"

Philippa looked back at Stella and then shrugged in agreement. They walked toward the laden spread, but they hit a snag halfway. Mickey had seen the bar.

"Let's get a little more champagne, whaddaya say?"

Philippa rolled her eyes like she'd seen it all before—because she had—and then nodded happily and said, "Okay, Mickey, it's your night. Order 'em up."

They moved toward the bar but soon discovered that the bartender was distracted by a burly older man who spoke in a pretentious, nasally tone. His lips smacked together wetly to punctuate every word.

"Are you a barkeep?" he was saying. "And do you know your trade?"

The girl in the bow tie behind the bar was stammering something. It was a painful sight for Mickey to watch. If there was anything he hated more than waiting on a drink, it was watching a blowhard pick on working girls. "It's just that . . . ," she said timidly.

"Well, then, I don't understand why you can't make

me a simple, little cocktail. A *sidecar*. It's a very simple drink, really. Cognac, orange liqueur, lemon, sugar . . ."

"'Scuse me," Mickey said, stepping in front of the guy. "I'm Mickey Pardo, art star. Maybe you've heard of me?"

The older man shook his head. Mickey couldn't tell if the man was sneering or if that was just the way his face always looked.

"Now I know you're a liar. But whatever. You want to tell me what the problem is?" Mickey could feel Philippa's hand on his arm, telling him to go slow.

"Certainly," the man said impatiently. "I'd like a sidecar. This young woman calls herself a bartender, yet she won't make me one. That's my problem. Which, incidentally, is none of your business."

Mickey looked at the bartender, who winced apologetically. "It's just that we don't have hard alcohol tonight, just wine, beer, and . . ."

Mickey nodded at the girl. "Listen Mister," he said turning to the man. "I'm not sure where you get off, but nobody talks to girls who serve me drinks that way. You'll drink champagne like everybody else, and you'll like it!"

The bartender poured a glass of champagne and handed it to the man, smiling sarcastically. The man had gone pale, but he just took his flute and stepped away.

"Two champ-pagnies," Mickey said, now that he had the bar to himself.

"Thanks for that," the bartender said, as she filled two flutes.

"Don't mention it, sister," Mickey said, taking the glasses and handing one to Philippa. As they clinked a toast she rolled her eyes affectionately. For a moment it was like they were a couple again and she was embarrassed by her jackass of a boyfriend. It was the sweetest moment Mickey'd had all week.

meanwhile, back in the west village . . .

"What do you think you want to see, Sara-Beth?" Hilary Grobart said patiently. They were standing in front of the Quad Cinema on Thirteenth Street.

Sara-Beth tilted her head and ruffled her hair. "I'm not sure, I guess. What movie do you think I want to see?"

"The Kate Winslet costume drama looks like a good movie," Hilary said. "And she's such a brilliant actress."

Sara-Beth's eyes got very large and dewy.

"But on the other hand," Sam Grobart said quickly, "you've had a very difficult week, and there's no sense in sitting through a long, boring movie set in the nine-teenth century, am I right? How about the Brad Pitt action flick, eh?"

"Yes, that's what I'd like to see," Sara-Beth agreed.

David was half paying attention to this exchange, and half paying attention to the crowd of polite but curious onlookers who had gathered on the sidewalk.

"That's an excellent choice, sweetheart," Hilary said

"SBB, SBB," one of the girls in the gathering crowd called, "what are you doing? Is this your family?"

Sara-Beth looked up at the Grobarts with a face of trepidation. David saw, again, that exposed helplessness and raw emotion and he was seized with a desire to take her home and cuddle. Then she turned, put on a radiant smile, grabbed David by one hand and Hilary by the other. She stepped toward her fans.

"Hey people!" she called, in a voice that sounded much more happy-go-lucky than anything David had ever heard her utter before. "What's going on?"

"What are you doing here?" said a girl who looked about ten. She was staring in awe.

"Well, cute-stuff, I'm having a very low-key evening with my new adoptive family, the Grobarts. That's Hilary, and that's Sam—aren't they just the nicest-looking ever?"

The camera phones started coming out, and everyone was taking pictures. Several girls passed celebrity weekly magazines up to Sara-Beth, and she signed them happily.

"Thanks, Suzy," she was saying, and, "Oh, that's so sweet of you. I'm so glad you're my fan!"

The warm night and the adulation of the masses wrapped around the Grobarts. David eyed his parents, who looked a little awkward but mostly just proud.

They were holding hands and watching quietly. With their matching windbreakers on they looked a little bit like body guards. David wondered if maybe this wasn't one of those moments they were always talking about that brought families closer together.

"And this," Sara-Beth said, drawing David forward, "Is my new boyfriend, David." She made a thumbs-up motion at the crowd and said, "Isn't he cute?!"

The crowd did seem to think David was cute. They called out to him to pose, and then several of them wanted David's autograph, too. Sara-Beth put her arms around his waist and squeezed him; the crowd gasped with pleasure. David couldn't believe this was happening to him, and he tried to take in as much of it as possible while he could.

Eventually, Hilary leaned in and whispered to Sara-Beth, "Is this getting maybe a little exhausting for you? Perhaps we should go in and find our seats."

Sara-Beth looked up at her and nodded, although she didn't move to do anything. She just held onto David's hand and reached for Hilary's.

"All right, thank you everyone," Hilary said sternly to the crowd. "Sara-Beth appreciates all your good wishes, but we're going to go be normal now. All right?"

Some of the girls called out for more autographs, but Sam gently told them no, and then ushered his wife, son, and newest patient toward the movie theater entrance.

As David reached the door, he saw his friend Patch zooming down Thirteenth Street on his skateboard, looking really . . . upset. David turned and watched him go down the wide street, and just before he disappeared, David saw what he thought was a cell phone getting hurled into the passing traffic.

"David," Sara-Beth called, and he followed her clacking heels in to get seats for the new Brad Pitt action movie.

I'd been having bad dreams that I couldn't remember upon waking, and by midweek, I was feeling pretty rattled. So I took myself to the movies.

There was a documentary about subsistence farmers in Guatemala playing at the Angelika, the art house theater on Broadway and Houston, so I went there and got myself a big popcorn and a small Coke and settled in.

Of course, just when you start feeling really introspective and low, that's when New York comes crashing in on you like a small town. I had barely eaten my first pieces of popcorn when a girlish voice somewhere close behind me whispered, "Hey, Jonathan!"

I turned around, and there was Lily Maynard, with her moon face and shiny brown hair. She looked more happy than surprised to see me, which was a surprise. "Hey, Lily."

"I'm so excited about this movie, aren't you?" she said, giving me a kind of weird look.

"Yeah," I said. "It's a topic I've always been interested in."

She gave me a big smile and waggled her fingers at me, and then went back to her Junior Mints. But it took me the first half of the movie to forget that an actual do-gooder was sitting three rows behind me.

Eventually, though, the images of the lush *fincas*, the bright-colored clothes of the workers, and the soft but determined voiceover of the translator lulled me, and I stopped thinking about Lily Maynard, and I started thinking about my stalling efforts to recreate myself. What was my problem, after all? I knew what it was, deep down.

I was afraid of the community garden.

After all, I had fully intended to donate my clothes to the Salvation Army, and they were still sitting in the foyer doing nobody any good. And I had also meant to start donating money to homeless people on the street, but I was so used to ignoring them that I kept forgetting. What made me think that I would be any better at gardening?

The thing is, I'm finicky. I always have been, and even though I knew this was going to be a really

189

great thing to be involved with, I was doubting my ability to get down in the mud. And the dirt. And work.

I thought about this for the rest of the documentary. Finally, it ended, with a helicopter shot of forests and the dramatic score rising and filling the nearly empty theater. I snuck out before the credits so as not to have to talk to Lily Maynard, and then I walked downtown in a hurry because I was afraid I might run into her again.

I thought and walked, moving downtown with my hands stuffed into my pants pockets. And then I saw something that pushed my thinking in an entirely different direction.

There, in front of the Quad theater, was a crowd of screaming preteen girls. They were standing around gasping over a little starlet and a tall, dark-haired guy. The object of the crowd's affection, I realized after a few beats, was Sara-Beth Benny, and the handsome dude at her side was David. They were climbing into a cab, heading back downtown, and one young girl had thrown herself in front of the car.

This was one of those scenes that makes the world you live in every day seem foreign all of a sudden.

Then I remembered seeing David and Sara-Beth together, as though in a dream, at a diner in Vassar. I realized with a chill that I hadn't talked to David since last weekend, when we all drove up north, and that fact was so weird in and of itself that I couldn't do anything but keep on walking.

Mickey woke up unusually early on Thursday morning, having slept just over two hours, because yet another irresistible invitation had been extended to him the night before at the Met. Porter Aronsky, the dashing financier and art collector, had invited him for a morning spin around the island on his yacht. He had actually called Manhattan the island, and he had actually referred to the proposed trip as a spin. Mickey admired that kind of flair and had said yes immediately. He dressed quickly and was almost out the door when he heard a familiar voice whisper, "Where do you think you're going?"

Mickey hadn't seen seven o'clock in quite a while, and he hadn't anticipated anybody else being up in the Pardo house, either. But there was Caselli, ready for him at the door. Mickey smiled weakly at his minder, hoping he didn't look as disheveled as he felt. "I'm going for a *spin* around the *island,*" he said, wondering as the words spilled out of his mouth if he were still drunk. "At least, I think I am."

"Oh, no you're not." Caselli crossed his arms over his chest, looking all of a sudden very much like Mr. Clean. "Even art stars have to go to school."

A shower, a change of clothes, and a pot of black coffee later, Mickey was being deposited from the back of Caselli's Triumph at the door of Elizabeth Irwin.

"Thanks, man," Mickey said.

"Bye, Mickster."

Mickey watched Caselli ride off. Just as he was admitting to himself that it was too late to catch the spin around the island, his cell phone started buzzing in his pocket. He was surprised it still had juice, but even more surprised that Philippa's name was in the caller ID box.

"I can't believe you're up already, too," Mickey said by way of hello.

"Mickey?" Philippa said. The urgency in her voice socked him with a sudden need to be very close to his ex-girlfriend. "I need to see you now."

"Whoa, sister," Mickey said. "It's going to take me at least five minutes to get to wherever you are."

"I'm at Doma."

"Give me five."

When Mickey walked into the West Village café, it took him a moment to spot Philippa, because she was sitting in the corner and wearing a gigantic gray cashmere turtleneck that might also have been worn as a dress. Her hair was pulled back in a neat ponytail, and she wasn't wearing any makeup.

Mickey kissed her on the cheek and sat down across from her.

"You were in rare form last night," she said.

"It was really fun hanging out with you." Philippa turned her face away from him, and gave the street a long, pensive look. "So what did you need to see me about so urgently?"

Philippa collected herself for a moment, and then said, "My parents heard about the pictures."

"Which pictures?"

"Your pictures. The naked pictures. They haven't seen them, but they know about them from their friends. They heard I was posing with a bunch of lesbians."

"Well, that can't really shock them now. Right?"

"Um," Philippa tugged the neck of her turtleneck up around her chin. "I haven't really told them yet. I know, I know. I seem all rebellious, but . . . I just couldn't. I will, but I can't yet."

"They haven't met Stella?"

"They think she's my SAT tutor."

"Oh. Wow."

"Mickey, the thing is, you can't show those pictures anymore. That thing you did at Vassar just blew up, and I know you were planning to do it again this weekend.

But you can't show those photos again. If my parents keep hearing these rumors, they'll start thinking it's true. And then they'll know."

Mickey looked at his ex-girlfriend and tried to deal with the fact that what she was saying wasn't a prelude to asking if he wanted to get back together. For a moment he was afraid she might cry, but then she didn't. She just said, "Do it for me, okay? Retire the naked pictures."

Mickey saw his whole art career flash before his eyes. He stopped thinking about the fact that Philippa didn't want to get back with him, and started thinking about the fact that all week he had been riding on one fluke accomplishment. "But what am I going to talk about at Sarah Lawrence?"

Philippa just stared at him with her wide, pale eyes.

"Okay," he said. "Okay. I won't show the naked pictures anymore."

"Good. And you never know, maybe this will lead you to do something even better."

"You think I can start over again? With photography?"

Philippa gave Mickey a twisted, adorable smile. "Maybe you're about to take the best pictures of your life."

The balmy warmth of California made Patch feel better almost instantly, although as he approached the ranch he was still wracked by some pretty big emotions, like anger and confusion, that he didn't experience very often.

After Greta had confessed to cheating on him with her ex-boyfriend and promised that it didn't mean anything and that she still wanted to be with him if he could forgive her, Patch had said he was going to have to think about it and call her back in a few hours. He still hadn't figured out how he felt about it, which was why he still hadn't called her back.

As he walked onto the campus of his Uncle Heyday's alma mater, he was struck by how different Deep Springs was from Vassar. The buildings weren't grand, and they were mostly just one-story, but the chalky foothills rising up in the background were definitely impressive. It might have been that Patch had taken the red-eye flight from JFK, but the vastness of the sky and the mountains struck him as really awe-inspiring.

It was also weird how much activity was going on for such an early hour. Young men seemed to be dragging farm equipment every way he looked. As Patch approached the low-lying ranch building at the center of campus, he saw a guy about his age plucking at a banjo.

"Hi," Patch said once he was close enough to be heard. He took off his Yankees hat and stuffed it in a pocket of his worn corduroys.

"Hi," the guy said. He was tall and tanned, with broad shoulders and light blond hair that rendered his eyebrows and eyelashes practically invisible. There was something Vikinglike about him, and as he looked up at the visitor, he didn't exhibit any signs of curiosity, excitement, or irritation. He didn't look like a guy who got irritated about much.

"I'm here to visit your school," he said. "My name's Patch. I'm from New York."

"Where's that?" the guy said.

"It's, um—"

"I'm just kidding, I know where it is. New Yorkers are sort of like Deep Springers, actually. We all think we live in the center of the universe."

Patch nodded. "I'll buy that. Man, it smells good here."

"Yeah, takes the new guys a while to get used to it."

Patch turned to survey the ranch. There were a few, faint stars in the patch of lavender sky at the top of the mountains. "A lot of activity for such an early hour."

"It ain't easy, going to Deep Springs."

"Doesn't seem like a regular college at all."

"But you come to love it. Me, I'm dairy boy this semester, so I have to be at work with the cows by six. But last night I was up all night reading Heidegger, so I haven't slept much." The guy plucked the banjo for emphasis. "Just waiting on breakfast right now. Mario's preparing the fixings. Can you smell it?"

"Not really," Patch admitted. "Mostly it's just alfalfa and mud that I smell right now. But it's all new to me, and I haven't slept much, either. What did you say your name was?"

"Recently, people have been calling me Dairy Boy. I have a real name, too, but for now you can just call me Dairy Boy. I don't really want a name to come between me and my identity as a worker."

"Okay," Patch said. It was weird how little this guy seemed to care about talking to him, although after all the unwanted attention he'd been getting in New York, he couldn't say he minded. "Hey, I'm looking for the admissions office. Is it in here?"

"There's no admissions office as such," Dairy Boy

said. "But most of the administrative stuff gets done in there, yeah."

"Thanks," Patch said.

"Hey man, you seem pretty far from home."

"True enough."

"Maybe you should come with us on our midnight hike tonight."

"Okay, I could do that."

"We'll go up into the foothills and build a fire. I'm going to bring my banjo. Maybe we can talk about what kind of home you're looking for."

As Patch headed into the building, he considered calling Greta. But deep down he knew that he still hurt too much to do that.

i discover a little-known creature
called the penguin

It started innocently enough. At lunch on Thursday, I met up with Arno and we got hotdogs and walked down Fifth Avenue.

"Where've you been, man?" I asked.

"I don't know. Around, I guess."

"Seems like everybody's been doing their own thing since we went to Vassar."

"Yeah, I guess that's true. Maybe we should all get together tonight?"

"Okay," I said. It was a nice gesture, Arno arranging the group hang and everything, but I was feeling too stressed about my stalling care campaign to really feel psyched about going out.

"I'm supposed to have dinner with that girl Gabrielle, the one we met Monday night, so it will have to be after that."

"Oh. Are you still in love with her?" I asked.

"I think the feeling might be fading. We're not

doing anything special, anyway, just dinner at Republic." Arno balled up the wax paper from his hot dog and threw it in a garbage can. "I guess it's time to go back, huh?"

"You go," I said.

"See you tonight?"

"Yeah."

I watched Arno walk back in the direction of Gissing, and then I continued down Fifth Avenue. I looked around me, but none of the people milling in the streets were familiar, so I cut over to Madison.

I walked by the Ralph Lauren store and looked in the windows for a moment. The mannequins were all wearing gorgeous, summery boating wear. Finally, I couldn't stand it anymore. I went in. And I shopped. And when I was done with Ralph Lauren, I went to Lacoste, and then Thomas Pink. God help me, I went to Barneys.

A few hours later, I emerged from Barneys feeling foggy and low. It felt like I'd really done lasting damage in the quest to recreate myself. I swung my shopping bags in irritation as I walked back up Fifth, dwarfed by all those consumerist havens.

"Save the penguins?" A timid voice said.

I looked, through bleary eyes. A slender guy in a

yellow T-shirt was standing in front of me with a clipboard. "Excuse me?"

"There are nineteen species of penguins in the world, and eleven of them are in danger of becoming extinct. Would you like to help save the penguins?"

"Yeah," I said. "Yes. That sounds like an important cause. A cause I could care about. Care about *tremendously*. What can I do?"

"Well, I work for Greenpeace, and I'm trying to collect signatures for this petition. We're trying to legislate various protections for Alaskan penguins. The way it works is—"

"I'll sign," I said quickly. "I'll sign twice. Once for me and once for a friend."

"Once is good," the guy said, handing me the clipboard. I signed, and handed it back to him. "Thanks."

"Thank *you*," I said. We both stood there awkwardly, and when I realized that I was the one who was supposed to move first I waved and walked uptown through the crowd. There, I thought. I did a good deed, and I didn't even get my hands dirty.

I pushed through the crowd, figuring I could at least make my last class. There were a lot of tourists on the street, though, not moving and staring up at the building façades or whatever.

Suddenly I pushed into a short woman in a yellow T-shirt.

"Sorry, sorry," I said.

"That's okay," she said. "Care to save the penguins today?"

I paused for a moment. The woman had thick black bangs and a prominent chest that I'd run right into, and her voice was definitely not timid. "Yes," I said. "Yes I would care to save the penguins." I figured I'd sign Patch's name.

"You're one of the good ones, sir. We're trying to legislate protections for Alaskan penguins—there are a variety of species of penguin and many of them are endangered."

"That's awful," I said. "I had no idea."

As I signed the petition on her clipboard, she continued to rattle off facts about the plight of the penguin. I started to be genuinely touched by her cause. I mean, those poor, adorable penguins. They waddle, for Christ's sake.

"You really seem to care," the girl said, after I had taken in her speech.

"Really?"

"Most people won't even stop to talk to me."

"I mean, who doesn't care about penguins?"

"I know! But even the people who stop don't

listen like you do. Maybe you would like to make a monetary donation to Greenpeace? We can arrange to have a small amount—say, ten dollars—taken out of your account at the beginning of each month. Of which one hundred percent would go to saving endangered species."

I agreed immediately and filled out the form, carefully writing down the numbers on my bankcard.

"You'll get newsletters and stuff, too."

"Great," I said.

"Thank you for caring so much," she said.

Those words stayed with me as I turned away and headed uptown. I knew it wasn't much, but I felt like I had taken a few itty-bitty steps toward my redemption.

There were three more Greenpeace volunteers between Barneys and Gissing, and I signed petitions for them all. The last one was so impressed with my caring that she asked me if I wanted to become a "penguin buddy" by donating three hundred dollars to the cause. I agreed immediately. The best part was that all of the "penguin buddies" got front row seats for a lecture that night on the plight of the species. I was going to meet lots of other people who cared about penguins, too!

david amidst the ghosts of the little screen

On Thursday afternoon, David didn't protest hard enough, and he was talked into a couple hours of pickup ball at the West Fourth courts. By the time he made it back to his apartment, he was feeling pretty guilty about leaving Sara-Beth with two middle-aged therapists for so long, and he wasn't even entirely sure why he'd done it.

Nobody seemed to have noticed his absence, though, and he was able to shower and get dressed without anybody paying attention to him. He could hear Sara-Beth and his parents talking giddily in the living room.

He waited in his bedroom for a little while, sort of looking at his homework and hoping that Sara-Beth would escape from his parents and come back and he could tell her about his day. Maybe she would ask him what kind of music she liked, and he would tell her that her favorite band was Arcade Fire because they were moody and refined, just like her. Finally he got sick of waiting and went to see what was going on.

Before he even set foot in the living room he knew it

was going to be strange, because the saccharine jingle of the hit TV show *Mike's Princesses* was playing from what sounded like an old, clunky cassette recorder. Cautiously, he peeked through the glass of the French doors. What he saw filled him with an icky, foreboding feeling.

They—his mother, his father, his girlfriend—were doing the dance routine that had opened each episode of *Mike's Princesses*. Of course, as far as David could remember, in the TV version, SBB and her costars had interacted with a bunch of animated flowers and bunnies and things. But the moves were distinctive enough.

"I'm Millie!" sang Sara-Beth, who was very much not six years old anymore. She did a twist, and a move with her arms, and then she came skidding in on her knees, singing, "I'm the youngest and the funnest and the one Mike loves the mostest!"

"I'm Tanya!" sang David's mom. Everyone always said that Hilary carried her weight well, and David had always thought this was true, too. Her curly hair was pulled back in a ponytail, but even so, doing a Charlestonlike move and smiling like a showgirl made her look old. And that made David sad. "I'm the smartest, most mature, the one boys on motorcycles pull over for!"

David realized simultaneously that this opening

sequence was geekier than most, and that he could not bare the sight of his father singing Courtney, the middle daughter's, part. Or Mike, the dad's, part, which would involved his swinging Hilary around and then kissing her on the forehead.

David walked in and hit stop on the cassette player, which he seemed to remember his father using to dictate portions of the unpublished novel he had been working on years ago. "What are you guys doing?" he asked.

"Oh, David!" his mother said, wiping a few beads of sweat from her face. David had to admit that she looked kind of exhilarated by whatever she had been doing. "Your father and I came up with this as an important step in Sara-Beth's recovery. You know, reliving 'the routine,' as they called it on set."

"But what about the day we met?" he asked Sara-Beth. "Don't you remember? You were so upset that those admissions people asked you to dance for them."

Sara-Beth stood up and ran her fingers through her hair. She was wearing on old gray sweatshirt of his and jeans rolled to mid-calf. She shrugged and looked at Hilary.

"During our session yesterday, Sara-Beth told us that this sequence recurred in her dreams, that it in effect haunted her. Well, we are exorcising it, if you will. This is a way to rid the opening dance sequence of any negative content. We are making it a happy thing, and we probably will have to do it many more times again before it loses its power over our young Miss Benny."

"David, don't look so skeptical," his dad said. Sam Grobart was wearing an old T-shirt and sweats, which made David feel even more icky for some reason. "The opening song and dance sequence is a metaphor for the entire show, of course, and maybe for Sara-Beth's whole career. This show-biz-esque routine really contains every wrong inflicted on a child actor."

Sara-Beth nodded at him, and smiled. "Don't worry about me David, really. What your parents are doing for me is so wonderful and positive. I'm not as fragile as you think, you know."

David nodded helplessly, as his girlfriend of a few days turned to his parents, clapped her hands, and said, "Let's take it from the top."

Before he was exposed to any more, David retreated to his room. As soon as the door was shut behind him, he called Jonathan.

"Hey man," Jonathan said, picking up after the fourth ring.

"Hey."

"What's going on, dude?"

"Oh, I just . . . Well, Arno called me earlier. He said that we were all meeting at some dive bar off Union

Square to hang tonight. You going?"

"Um, maybe. Actually, I'll be there, but really late. Something's come up . . . I'll tell you about it later if I make it."

"Oh . . . okay. Hey, can I ask you something?"

"Does it have to do with penguins?"

"No, I guess not."

"Oh. Oh well. Fire away."

"If a guy . . . say a guy, like, our age, had a girlfriend, let's say, like, a pretty new girlfriend, do you think it would be weird if that guy's parents took a really big interest in the emotional life of the girlfriend? Do you think that would make the whole thing a little . . . incestuous?"

"How new is the girlfriend?" Jonathan asked.

"Let's say under a week."

"Huh. Yeah, I'd say that would be weird. You want to hear something tragic though?"

"Guess so."

"There are nineteen species of penguins, and eleven of them are endangered. Doesn't that just blow your mind? Penguins, those adorable little tuxedo-wearing, waddling birds. They are birds, right?"

"Yeah, pretty sure."

"Hey David, I gotta go. But I'll try to come by tonight . . . But you know, I gotta help those little penguins."

"Yeah, man," David said. He really hoped he'd see Jonathan later—Jonathan was very good at undoing romantic entanglements.

"And David? Promise me that you'll send good thoughts to the penguins, okay?"

arno gets some advice, and gives some

"Jonathan double-booked us?" Mickey said sadly.

"Yeah," David said, still not quite believing it.

"Whatever," Arno said. They were sitting in one of the dark booths, in the back of a skuzzy bar they usually only went to before going to shows at Irving Plaza. There was only one girl in the bar, and she was dancing by herself to the White Stripes song that had been playing everywhere for the last two weeks.

"What have you guys been doing?" David asked, lounging back in the booth and running his hand over his nearly bare head. "I feel like I've been trapped in my own little world for the last week."

"What, you haven't read about your famous friend Mickey in the papers?" Mickey said, smiling devilishly. He was wearing a black poncho and his hair had grown as wild as his eyes. "Joking, man. I'm not that bad yet, referring to myself in the third person and shit."

"That would be lame," Arno agreed.

"Yeah. Anyway, you won't believe it, but I've been third-wheeling it with Philippa."

"You mean Philippa has a"—David closed his eyes while he said it—"girlfriend?"

"Yup. Her name's Stella. She's okay, actually, and she writes about art for her college paper. We've been going to mostly art-related shit, for obvious reasons," Mickey sighed. "Only problem is, I really started thinking Philippa and I were going to get back together."

"What?" Arno said. "Man, you've got to stop thinking about your ex. I mean, we're going to Sarah Lawrence this weekend, right? Get a little more college in our lives? And you're giving another lecture, so girls are going to be all over you. Stop thinking about her *now*."

"Yeah . . . ," Mickey said, his eyes glazing over with either anticipation or regret. "Hey, speaking of Sarah Lawrence girls, don't you have a little lady waiting there for you, too?"

Arno sank back against the creaky wood paneling of the booth and brushed his bangs out of his eyes dreamily. "Lara . . . yeah. I haven't talked to her since last Saturday, but I've spent the week putting everything, like, in place for us to get together this weekend. She's just like everything I ever wanted, you know?"

"Mmm . . . ," Mickey said.

"I do feel a little bad," Arno went on slowly, watching the other guys for a reaction, "cuz I've been seeing someone else."

"So?" David said. Then he remembered Sara-Beth calling him Arno, and he was hit with a sudden wave of paranoia. "Who is she?"

"This girl Gabrielle. I met her on Monday when Jonathan and I went to this theater benefit."

"Gabby Mercy?" Mickey asked.

"You know her?" Arno said dully. He realized he didn't even know Gabby's last name.

"Sweet Mercy Theater Company?" Mickey laughed. "She's a sophomore at Adele Biggs, dude."

"Oh."

"Listen, she's cute and everything, but she's a little . . ." Mickey made a circling motion by his ear, "cuckoo, you know what I mean? Listen, you were in L-O-V-E with this Sarah Lawrence person. You just said she was everything you've ever wanted. Why not hold out for the best?"

"Thanks man, I'm glad you think so," Arno said, because that was exactly what he was going to do anyway.

"But listen, about this Sarah Lawrence thing? There's a hitch."

"Yeah?"

"Yeah. I can't show the pictures anymore."

"You mean, the pictures that made David famous with the ladies?" Arno asked. Even in the reddish light, he saw David blush a little bit.

"Yeah, long story, but I promised someone important that I'd retire them."

"Wow."

"It's okay, though. I just have to take new photos. The lecture was pretty much freestyle last time anyway, so I'm not worried about that."

"What are you going to do?" David asked.

"Tell me what you think. Be brutally honest. I'm going to do New York at dawn, with one, lone naked figure dashing through. You know, architecture of the city, architecture of the body. Brick and steel vs. flesh and bone. Man vs. industry. Plus, it's like a whole different way of looking at our urban landscape."

"Oh, that's *cool*," Arno said enthusiastically.

"Who's the one lone figure?"

"Oh, well, me of course."

"I think that's awesome," David said. "The first project was great, but a little too much like that Luc Vogel guy. This will be so much more personal."

Arno nodded in agreement.

"Can we talk about this girl thing again though?" David said.

214

Arno raised an eyebrow, and Mickey finished his beer. Luckily, they had ordered two of everything.

"See, I met this girl at Vassar. And we've been dating since. Well, *living* together is more like it, I guess. And she has some problems. She was on this TV show when we were kids? *Mike's Princesses*? Sara-Beth Benny?"

Mickey spit out his beer. "*You're* dating SBB?"

"Yeah, we all know her. We hung out with her on that cruise ship, remember? Oh, wait, I guess it was after you got kicked off . . ." Arno looked uncomfortable. "What do you mean, living together?"

"I guess she was really lonely in her penthouse. So she's been staying at my place. And hanging out with my parents. A little bit too much."

"Whoa," Arno said. Then he clinked beers with David. "Way to go. That's hot."

"But it's not that hot. I mean, it's like having a really cute sister sort of, because my parents are treating her now and it's like every moment we spend together is family therapy hour," David paused. "I mean it's not *always* like she's my sister. But the parent thing . . . do you think it's a little weird?"

Mickey shook his head. "She's hot, man. Who cares if she's your sister?" When he saw David's face he added, "That was a joke, man."

"Listen," Arno said, "famous people are always

susceptible to group therapy and cults and stuff like that. She'll get over it, or maybe you'll get over her. But in the meantime, Mickey's right, she's hot, and she can get you in anywhere. You should go with it, you know? Have fun. She totally raises your stock."

"Not that it wasn't on the rise anyway," Mickey put in.

"You think I should keep living with her?"

"Definitely," Mickey said.

"You think I should stop feeling bad about this Gabby chick, and go for it with Lara?" Arno asked.

"Totally."

"You think I should make my name with a naked at dawn in New York City photo series, starring moi?"

"Abso-freaking-lutely."

"For me it was Athens, 2004—that was when I knew," said Brendan Lockheart, a second-year Deep Springs student with sandy hair and shoulders still broad from his stint as an Olympic swimmer. Like a lot of the guys sitting around the fire, he was wearing a flannel button-up shirt and corduroys that looked like they got worn in the classroom as well as in the wilderness. "I had just won the gold in the 400 meter butterfly, and it should have been huge. But I realized that I had just been living off insane luck and charm and all this weird adoration. I mean, my life was just empty ambition. I had no idea how to work for something or think anything through. Then someone told me about Deep Springs, so I dropped out of Yale and applied. Best thing I've ever done."

The other guys nodded. There were about ten of them—they had hiked off the ranch after dinner and walked two hours or so before stopping to build a fire. Everything around them was very dark and very quiet.

Patch poked at the embers of the fire with his walking stick and listened.

"So, Patch," Dairy Boy said eventually. He was sitting next to Patch on the ground and occasionally plucking at his banjo. "What brought you to Deep Springs?"

Patch was almost surprised to hear his name. The guys had hiked in near silence, and no one had seemed particularly interested in who he was or what he was doing there. Patch had enjoyed the ruminative privacy these guys seemed to exist in, but the question Dairy Boy had put to him didn't feel particularly invasive, either.

"I was thinking about going to all these schools on the East Coast, the same ones my New York guys are considering. But in the city I get all this weird attention. It's like everybody thinks they know who I am, and they want a piece of that. I don't know if I can handle another four years of living with other people's perceptions of me."

Dairy Boy let out a soft chuckle. Patch thought he was going to tell him to get over himself for a moment. "I've been there, man," Dairy Boy said. "It's really hard to get into this school, so, you know, don't assume anything. But you're going to hear a lot of similar stories from the other guys here—a lot of us have dealt with that same situation, and Deep Springs helped us get away from the oppressive attention of the rest of the world. This might be the one place where you could self-actualize, instead of being tugged down by the way everybody else deals with your, like . . . Patchness."

The other guys made mumbling agreement sounds.

Patch nodded. That sounded right on to him—it was, in fact, what he had been thinking about for the entire hike. "There's one hitch, though. My girlfriend and I were planning on going to the same school. She's from out west, so this is our chance to be together."

"Every story needs a girl," Brendan said philosophically.

Patch nodded. He wondered what Greta was doing right now. The fire snapped, and the stars shown above him. Patch knew that she was sorry, but it didn't really matter anymore, because he knew he wasn't going to choose a college that both of them could go to. He was going to choose Deep Springs.

all mickey wants from his papa is a nice, warm art crit

"Dad? *Daaaad*?" Mickey knocked on the worn metal door to his dad's office. He knew Ricardo was in there because the lights were on and because he could smell cigar smoke wafting under the door. He hadn't felt quite so like a child since he was one. "Dad," he whined, "I know you're there!"

He was standing in the hall in his dad's old, white terry-cloth robe, and he was holding a box of negatives. Caselli had developed them as soon as Mickey got home from his dawn tour of the city. Now, still exhilarated from the dewy jaunt, as well as from having escaped a citation for indecent exposure, Mickey wanted nothing so much as to show off the results.

"Paaaaa-*piiiii*!" he cried. That must have carried, because Mickey heard the sound of a chair scraping across the floor and a few seconds later Ricardo's face appeared in the crack of the doorjamb.

"Yes, what do you want?" Ricardo said tightly.

"Yo, dad." Mickey took a deep breath. "Listen, I know you weren't crazy about my last big splash in the art world. But I'm giving another lecture tomorrow night, and I thought I'd do something new."

Ricardo turned down both ends of his mouth, and nodded. "Impressive. The great Mickey Pardo thinks he actually needs to do something new."

Mickey watched his dad snarl a little as he said the word "new," and tried not to let it bother him. "Yup. I was hoping you would take a look at the new project? They're photos. I took them this morning. Maybe you could, you know, tell me what you think?"

Ricardo lowered his voice, keeping his evident fury close to his chest. "Get out of here *mijo*. Stop riling everybody up. Now you just do everything for show. Come back and talk to me about art when you've learned a little craft, eh?"

Then he slammed the heavy metal door in Mickey's face. Mickey turned and saw that Caselli was there waiting for him. "Come on, man," Caselli said. "Let me help you mount those slides for your lecture, okay?"

"Okay," Mickey said, walking back toward the photo studio with Caselli. He was trying hard to feel more pissed than hurt. "I don't see why he couldn't have just looked."

"Don't take it so hard, kiddo. I've been trying to get Ricardo to look at my stuff for years."

"That sucks."

"Yeah. And for what it's worth, I think your pictures are really sweet."

"Really?" Mickey said as they sat down at Caselli's worktable.

"Yeah. I especially like the one of you running through Battery Park with all the sailboats and, you know, New Jersey in the background. And going on a subway car was a really inspired move, too. There's something really brilliant and disturbed about that one."

"Thanks, man" Mickey said. He watched Caselli carefully cut the film and put each picture into little white slide mountings. He tried to remind himself of Arno and David's enthusiasm about the photos, and thought *to hell with you, Dad*. He stood up and paced a little circle around the center of the room.

"I'm Mickey Pardo," he muttered to himself, "and I'm doing it my way."

i finally get some answers

I hardly slept because of all the unanswered questions marching around in my head. Marching like the adorable little penguins in the film I'd stayed up most of the night watching after I got back from the penguin event. The most important question marching through my head, of course, was still whether or not I would be able to actually get down and put my hands in dirt. But I focused on another, also important question, instead.

What does a guy wear to his first community garden "work party"?

I decided—once I was actually awake, the sun was up and all of that, and I knew I was going to have to face my fate—that the best thing to do would be to dress just like Patch for my first community garden work party. I located my one pair of khakis, rolled them to the ankles, and put on these vintage Jack Purcell sneakers. Then I found an old T-shirt of my brother's, a green one, and put that on. I felt greener already.

I made myself a bowl of cereal and poured myself the rest of the pot of coffee that the house-keeper must have made that morning. I flipped through the paper just to remind myself that there's a lot of pain and suffering out there. And then, when I couldn't avoid it anymore, I grabbed a white canvas blazer off the rack by the door and headed for the far West Side.

There was already a lot of activity when I got to the site. I could see the other volunteers through the big open doors of the chain-link fence, pushing around wheelbarrows full of dirt and bending over to pat various green things. There were kids in there, too. I could hear them squealing. Somebody had brought a stereo, and it was currently playing that Modest Mouse song that got used in a car commercial.

I went up to the entrance and stood there sur-veying the scene. I felt like I was on the border of a magical realm or something, because everything beyond the chain-link fence was very green and despite all the activity, kind of calm. There was also a lot—I mean a *lot*—of dirt.

I stood there for a moment, looking at all the

people in their practical outfits working in very concentrated ways. Just when I was starting to worry that I might be a community garden work party wallflower, a girl walked up to me, looking pretty serious for a Friday at noon.

"Can I help you?" she asked. She had pale skin, but the brown freckles on her nose and cheeks made it a few shades darker, and she had really light-blue eyes. She was tall, almost as tall as I was, and thin, but not like I-don't-eat thin. She was wearing a navy-and-white striped polo T-shirt and beige capri pants, and she looked very Connecticut. But down-to-earth Connecticut.

I said the first thing that came into my head, which was, "Are you Lily Maynard's friend Ava?" I hadn't really expected Ava to be this pretty.

"No, I mean yes, well, I know her, you see what I mean?" The girl laughed and shook her head. "Man, I'm a geek. Yes. Yes! We're friends, and she's done a lot of work for the garden. She had all these great ideas about fundraisers so that we could buy equipment and bulbs and things. Pretty incredible, isn't it?"

"Yeah," I said. We both looked around to con- firm-slash-emphasize the "incredible" part.

"Don't take this the wrong way," the girl said,

"but you seem a little out of place." And then she laughed one of those too-loud, uncomfortable laughs that shows you how pretty a person's smile can be.

"It's my first time," I said. "I mean, I've never gardened before."

"Wow, really? Why don't you come with me then? I'm planting tomatoes over there." She pointed and I followed her as we walked through little rows of recently planted flowers and stalks. "What's your name, by the way," she said as she knelt down in the dirt.

"Jonathan," I said, hesitating. I hovered above her for a moment. I could smell that loamy garden smell, even from here. Ava looked up at me, shielding her eyes from the sun with a hand.

"I'll be there in a sec," I said, and then I was. I was kneeling in front of a little patch of soil, and I was ready to put a plant into the ground. "Okay. What do I do?"

Ava laughed. "Well, this is my little plot, and I'm planting heirloom tomatoes."

"Really? I love heirloom tomato salad."

"I know, aren't tomatoes wonderful? There's nothing as delicious as a homegrown tomato, don't you think? Hopefully, by the time fall rolls around, we'll be eating heirloom tomatoes all the time." Then she laughed that laugh again. "Man, that would be pretty boring if I really thought tomatoes were the most exciting thing in the world, huh?"

"I knew what you meant," I said, noticing that she had really full, healthy gums. "So, what do I do?"

"See these?" she pointed at a row of little cardboard planters. "These are seedlings that I planted a couple of weeks ago. They've just been growing by the window in my kitchen. Anyway, what you do is . . ." And then she showed me how to dig a little hole, water it, remove the seedling from its box, and reposition it the ground. "Go ahead and try one," she said when she was done.

We worked for a while, quietly putting the seedlings into rows in Ava's plot. Pretty soon there were two neat rows of heirloom tomatoes. It was actually really meditative, and for a while I lost myself in moving these delicate little living things from one home to another.

I was almost jolted when I heard Ava's voice saying, "That one's Brandywine."

"Huh?" I looked down at the seedling, with its couple of small leaves, in my hands.

"They all have these funny names. You know, like Kentucky Beefsteak and Green Zebra."

"Really? And I thought all there was to an heirloom tomato was eating."

She laughed at my not-very-funny joke. "So, where do you go to school?"

"Gissing. How about you?"

"Sutter-Gable. But I just started there junior year because my family moved from Boston. So, why was today the day you wanted to learn about gardening, Jonathan?" she asked, brushing her straight, healthy-looking hair behind her ear.

"Um," I stalled. Ava seemed like a person I could be honest with, but I figured half honesty was the way to go for the moment. "Well, I thought I should start caring about more diverse things."

"Oh really? What did you care about before?"

"Penguins, mostly. Did you know that there are nineteen species of penguins, and that eleven of them are endangered?"

"Yes, actually."

"Oh." I looked down at the knees of my pants, which were muddy from the dirt. Just then, a cloud went over the sun, and I saw Ava shiver. "Here," I said, grabbing the canvas blazer from where I'd left it on the ground. "Put this on."

She smiled. "Thanks, Jonathan. And thanks for helping me with my tomatoes."

"I'm really glad I did," I said. And then I realized that this was one of those moments when you have to make something happen. I knew I was supposed to be going to Sarah Lawrence with Mickey that night, but I felt like I really had to seize the moment. "Hey, do you want to do something tonight? There's this documentary playing at Film Forum that I kind of wanted to see, or . . ."

"Oh, I'd really like to," Ava said quickly, "but I'm going upstate this afternoon to visit Sarah Lawrence. My sister goes there, and I think it might be a really good place for me to go for college. But, could we maybe . . . I mean, was it just tonight, the documentary, or . . . ?"

"No, I don't really care about the documentary. I mean, I do *care* about the documentary. But really I'd just like to hang out with you sometime."

Ava smiled. "Okay."

"It's funny, because I was actually thinking about going to Sarah Lawrence this weekend." Man, that sounded like a lie. I smiled goofily.

"Oh really? Yeah, I'm seriously considering going there. Right now, it's between Reed, Oberlin, and Sarah Lawrence for me. But Sarah Lawrence has all these neat programs, like a Friday Night Cinema club. I think I'm going to check that out tonight. And you know it's William and Sarah Lawrence's old private estate, so there's a certain charm there."

"Yeah, I heard about that from my friend . . ."

I was about to tell her about Mickey when my cell phone went off in my pocket. It was ODB's "Got Your Number," which meant that it was the devil himself.

"Hey, dude," I said.

"Why aren't you here?" Mickey yelled.

"I'm . . ." I was about to explain, when I saw Lily Maynard charging at us through the garden. She was definitely coming in our direction and with a purpose. "I'll call you right back, okay?"

Lily stopped awkwardly when she saw Ava and me together. She was wearing her usual polar fleece jacket and these flared jeans that looked all wrong on her. If you've ever knelt in the dirt with someone, then you know it feels incriminating even when it isn't. "What's up?" I said guiltily. Why the hell was I feeling guilty? Then Lily laid it out for me.

"Jonathan, I've been thinking, about this whole Ted thing—and if he's taken, then maybe—I mean, if you wanted to—maybe *we* should go out?" she laughed awkwardly. "I mean, if I can't have the older brother, then . . ."

That was like an electric shock of freak the fuck out. It sent me to my feet. "Um, actually, I just talked to Ted last night about you. Turns out he just broke up with his girlfriend and he's always had a crush on *you*!"

Who was this maniac speaking through my body? Why was I trying to sabotage my brother? Ava was staring up at me like she was deeply confused. Damn, she had big, pretty eyes.

"Really?" Lily said. Her face was all sunshine now.

"Yeah, in fact, I have a phone date with him that I'm late for . . . to, you know, discuss his chances with you. See you later!" I waved at Lily and Ava, who were both staring at me in total confusion, and then I bolted right out of that community garden.

The first thing Arno knew was that he hadn't gone to bed until very, very late. The second was that the bed he was lying in was unfamiliar. Also, there were potted plants all along the windowsill just under where the light came slicing in.

Next to him, on the unfamiliar pillow, was a great mass of curling, golden hair. Arno picked up a pile of it and remembered where he was. He felt a smile spread across his face and a sudden urge to get out and seize his first day as a *real* grown-up. He had spent the night with Gabby. They had stayed up late talking and laughing and maybe even . . . falling in love. Mission accomplished.

"What's the matter, sugarplum, you all ready to run out?" Gabby said without looking up.

"What time do you think it is?"

"Way past first period."

Arno sat up and stretched. "Nice apartment," he said.

"You saw it last night, funny face."

Arno realized that was true, and nodded in agreement. The apartment was a big studio with high, black tin ceilings and a wall of exposed brick with a fireplace. There were several dress dummies in various corners, and one whole wall was covered with hanging hats.

Gabby rolled out of bed and went to put a kettle on the stove. She was wearing peach pajama shorts and a pajama top, and her hair seemed to catch every ray of light in the room.

"It's just really . . ." Arno flopped back in bed and tried to think of how to describe the place. "It's really, uh, *real* I guess."

Gabby smiled at him. "And I *really* live here! What a coincidence."

"Man, what time did we get home last night?"

Gabby shook her head at him and put her hands on her hips. "You called from the bar last night at like two-thirty. Me? I was just home, washing my hair. This behavior is enough to make me think you aren't really in love with me."

"Huh?"

Gabby was distracted by the kettle blowing, so she just gave him a mysterious smile and went back to the stove. She poured two cups of Irish Breakfast with milk and brought them over to the bed. She sat down next to Arno and kissed his cheek. Then she pigeon-toed her feet. "So . . . I know of a roof party tonight. I think it's going to be really gorgeous and clear today, so . . ."

Arno realized he was having trouble seeing straight, so he started focusing and refocusing his eyes. For a minute he thought what he was feeling might be early-onset heart disease, but then he realized that it was actually a yearning for something far away. But he had definitely done it now. He had been in love with somebody else, and he felt sure that if he found Lara now, she would let him be in love with her.

And today was the day he was going to Sarah Lawrence.

"Are you okay?" Gabby said. "If you don't want to go to the party . . ."

"No, the party's fine," Arno said, standing up and pulling on his pants. He tried not to look at Gabby as he buttoned his black, slim-fitting collared shirt. "I'll call you, okay?"

She grabbed his wrist and pulled him so that he bent down and kissed her on the mouth. Incredibly, she still tasted like artificial watermelon.

"See you," Arno called as he was reaching the door. Then he hustled down six flights of stairs and over to Mickey's house.

if mickey pardo's your guest, you send the limo

"Where are you? Naw, I think my cellie's screwed up. Would you just get over here?" Mickey gestured at Arno, who was pouring various liquids into a martini shaker, that he wanted one, too. Mickey was still wearing the white terry-cloth robe. "Because it's my lecture weekend. And Sarah Lawrence sent the limo. We're in it. So you'll be here? Soon? That soon? Okay, bye."

"Jonathan?" Arno asked, shaking the martinis and nodding toward the phone.

"Yeah, I thought he said he was *gardening* for a minute." They both laughed.

Mickey peered through the window of the limo and saw his father, who was sitting on the steps and glaring. He was chewing on the stump of a cigar and playing with a ball of clay.

"Your dad still raw about your newfound celebrity?"

"Yeah, he won't really talk to me."

"He'll get over it when he realises he's just being a

sore loser," Arno took a sip of his martini. "You know my dad says they've had calls from collectors about your work? People who used to be desperate to collect your dad's stuff." The Wildenburger Gallery had represented Ricardo's work since before Arno and Mickey were born.

"Really?"

"Yeah, I wasn't supposed to tell you. They're working out the kinks before they come to you with an offer. But just don't let the whole Ricardo thing bother you, you know what I mean?"

"Cheers to that," Mickey said. They clinked glasses.

Around the time they were making their second round of martinis, there was a knock on the window. Mickey rolled it down. "Yes?"

"Wow. No more puny rides from friends for you, huh?" Jonathan said.

"Pretty sweet, right?" Mickey opened the door. "Get in, man."

Jonathan crawled in. "Well, there's a lot more leg room in here than in the Mercedes, it's got that going for it," he said, settling into one of the plush bench seats.

"Man, you really *were* gardening."

"Yeah." Jonathan looked down at the brown spots on his knees and elbows and smiled. "I planted heirloom tomatoes."

"Do you need a change of clothes? I mean, we really gotta get this show on the road."

Jonathan shrugged. "Nah, it's cool. You don't mind, do you?"

"I don't mind, but *you* do," Mickey cackled. Then he got on the intercom and told the driver to hit it.

"So where are Patch and David?"

Arno grinned. "Man, you didn't hear about David? He's got a new girlfriend. You remember SBB? Sara-Beth Benny? The official policy is, we just leave him alone and let him enjoy it."

"SBB?" Jonathan asked. "You think that's a good idea?"

"Yes. *Hell* yes. She's *hot.*"

"And now that you mention it . . . I haven't seen Patch in a while," Mickey said.

"Well, it is Patch we're talking about here . . . ," Arno said, tossing his martini glass over his shoulder and switching to Bud Light.

"Thanks for reminding me about your lecture," Jonathan said, accepting a Bud Light from Arno. "I feel like a jerk for missing your last one. And Sarah Lawrence—I mean, what a coincidence." Jonathan smiled faintly to himself.

"Yeah," Arno agreed, smiling not so faintly. "It feels like fate, doesn't it?"

They all paused for a moment as the limo sailed uptown on the West Side highway, trying to locate just what the tug of fate feels like. Then, abruptly, the limo stopped.

Mickey got on the intercom. "What's the problem, Joey?"

"Must have been an accident, Mr. Mickey. Highway's blocked up far as I can see."

"Well, fine. Okay. Can't we just drive over all those people or something?"

"Hey, Mickey," Jonathan said. "Don't stress so much. Sarah Lawrence is like half an hour a way."

"How do you know?"

"At the community garden I met this girl whose older sister goes to Sarah Lawrence, and—"

"You know what J? You're right. I'm not going to stress so much. Arno, man, would you open another bottle of beer for me?"

Mickey rolled down his window and sucked in some breeze. That was when all of their cell phones buzzed simultaneously.

"New text," Jonathan said, taking his phone out of his pocket.

"You too?" Mickey said.

"Yeah," Arno said, flipping open his phone. "It's an S.O.S."

"You need to come get me *now*," David said into his cell phone as he hurried up Hudson.

"We'd come back downtown," Jonathan said. "Except right now we're kind of stalled in traffic on the West Side Highway."

"Really? Where at?"

"Um, just before the Seventy-second Street exit. Listen, what's this about?"

"Okay, don't go anywhere, okay?"

"David, I don't think—" David put his phone back in his pocket and waved his arms wildly at a passing taxi.

"I need you to take me to Seventy-second and Broadway as fast as humanly possible," David said. The driver gave him an irritated look in the mirror, but David just kept talking. "Take the streets. There's a traffic jam on the highway."

The driver took off up the avenues, and to David's amazement they hit a string of green lights that carried them nearly fifty blocks in no time. At the corner of

Seventy-second and Broadway, David tossed the guy a twenty and bolted.

David jogged down the hill and by the time he passed through the dog park before the highway, he was at a full run. A small dog yelped at him and then was restrained by its leash. David ran on, trying not to think of the utter stupidity of what he was about to do, and more about his dire need to be far, far away from Manhattan. It didn't take him long to reach his destination.

At Seventy-second he took one cautious look up the exit ramp, and after determining that there were no crazy drivers coming down toward him, he made a dash toward the roadway, hanging as close to the safety wall as he could.

When he made it up to the roadway, he saw that the traffic was indeed stalled and dense, with only a few cars moving a couple of inches at a time. But there was a breeze up there, and he could smell the Hudson. David felt sort of vulnerable and crazy, but also exhilarated, like he was the hero in a movie and he'd just outrun bad men driving Hummers.

He looked south but couldn't see the yellow Mercedes. A car horn blared ahead of him on the highway, and he followed its direction. A big, shiny white limo caught his eye. He paused, and the horn blared again, setting off all the other horns on all the cars on the highway. In the middle of the cacophony, Jonathan stepped out of the limo. "David! We're over here!"

David turned and trotted in the direction of the limo. Soon he was inside of it, where the AC was blasting and the drinks were cold.

"What happened to you?" Jonathan said. David stared at Jonathan and tried to figure out what was going on—his friend's hair was all tousled, and his clothes were rumpled, and he appeared to have several grass stains on his clothes.

"You want a beer?" Arno passed him a beer.

"Thanks, man. Are you guys still going to Sarah Lawrence?"

"No, we're just sitting in traffic for kicks," Mickey said. "Of course we're going to Sarah Lawrence. It's my lecture, yo."

"I know, I know," David said. "And now I can come."

"What *happened* to you?" Jonathan asked.

David took a swig of beer. Someone's phone was ringing. After a minute they realized it was Jonathan's. He held up his index finger and answered the phone with a low, "This is Jonathan."

"So where's SBB?" Mickey asked.

"Oh, man. It's too crazy to even . . ."

"What kind of charges?" Jonathan was saying.

David looked at Jonathan, who was covering one ear with his hand and listening to his cellphone with the other. "It all started yesterday, when I got home from school, and my parents and Sara-Beth were doing the routine."

"The routine?"

"Yeah, you know."

"From *Mike's Princesses*? The whole I'm Millie, I'm Tanya, I'm Courtney thing? Christ."

"How much was charged to Greenpeace?" Jonathan was saying into the phone.

"Apparently it's part of her therapy. Getting out the bad feelings or something. Anyway, I got away from it and decided that if that's what she needed I should just let it happen, you know? But when I got home today they were doing it and they told me—"

"What, what?"

"—that they needed a person to do Mike's part. That this was something we had to do as a *family*."

"No way," Mickey said. "The whole swinging-them-around thing?"

Jonathan shushed them, so they lowered their voices.

"You didn't do it, did you?" Arno whispered.

"No way." David shook his head like he still couldn't believe it. "*Now* do you understand why I had to run up a freeway off-ramp to find you?"

Mickey and Arno nodded. "You can't date your fake sister," Arno said woefully.

"I appreciate the call, but I think those charges are all correct," Jonathan was saying. "I know, it *was* a big spending day for me. Thanks so much." He hung up and rolled his eyes at his friends. "I mean, how much do I spend on clothes, and Chase needs to call me about a donation to Greenpeace? Sheesh."

The guys all gave him bemused looks.

"So, David, what the hell happened, man?"

David spread his long legs and leaned back in his seat. "Can I tell you later, dude? I just want to stop thinking about it for a minute."

"Okay," Jonathan said. Then his phone rang again. "This is Jonathan," he said into the receiver, waving apologetically at David. "Oh hey, Ted . . . Yeah, man, it was amazing seeing you too. Well, the thing is . . . do you remember this Lily Maynard girl?"

"So how'd the new photos come out?" David asked Mickey.

"Oh, they're freaking awesome!" he replied.

"I know. I know I shouldn't have done that," Jonathan was saying.

"You gonna change up your lecture at all?" Arno asked.

"Nah, freestyle worked last time," Mickey said,

confidently rearranging his robe. Finally the traffic had started to move.

"No, I think I'm into this other girl . . . yeah, she's a real do-gooder . . . well, you know, but I want you to meet her . . . so you'll call her and straighten it out?" Jonathan was saying into his phone. "Man, you're the best. I'll call you soon, okay? Bye." He let out a sigh and turned to his friends. "Can you guys not wait until high school is over and we can just be in college already or what?"

Patch laid down his backpack in front of the office and knocked on the door.

A few moments passed, and then he knocked again. Just when he thought he might have the wrong place, he heard a loud "Yuuuuup?!" from the other side of the door. Patch pushed it open and took a look inside.

In the center of the small, blond-wood paneled office was a very tall man in a faded denim shirt. He was slim, but he had the kind of chest and shoulders that suggest a lifetime of athleticism. He had long fingers, which he laced together and positioned as a headrest as he looked up expectantly at Patch. "Yes, young man?"

"Hey, are you Richard Sorrel? I mean, President Sorrel," Patch said. He could see, through the office's one large window, a lot of the guys from the hike last night doing their afternoon chores. Then sun was glinting like gold in the hay out there, and Patch felt sure he was going to take that image back to New York with him.

"Dick! Call me Dick. Have a seat?"

"Thanks, man. Um, I'm Patch Flood, and I've been visiting the school the last couple of days and . . ."

Dick's smile faded. "You seem like a very nice young man. But I just want to warn you, ours is a very tough admissions process."

"Oh, yeah. I know. I just wanted to introduce myself because I think this might be the right place for me. My uncle Heyday—Heyday Flood?—went here and . . ."

"Deep Springs does not have a legacy program, young man," Dick said sternly. He scratched the stubble on his beard and cocked an eyebrow as though he were trying to categorize Patch as *us* or *them*.

"I know, I think that's really cool," Patch said, liking the dude and the school more every second.

"It's a lot of work, going to a school like this." Dick rested his mighty elbows on the desk and looked deep into Patch's eyes.

"I'm down for a lot of work. My life in New York's sort of coasting, you know? I've done that."

"Young man," Dick said, craning back so that his chair stood on two legs, and propping his cowboy boots on the table, "when I was your age, I had already taught English in Japan and mined for gold in Africa. Life is an adventure, but that doesn't mean there shouldn't be roots, a history of hard work in one place, friends who understand you and are as tough on you as you are on yourself. That's what this school is about, so don't apply if you just want something eclectic on your c.v., understand? Life should be about something," Dick paused for effect and let the front legs of the chair come crashing down on the wood floor. "That's what we teach."

Patch stood and nodded. He shook the guy's hand. "That all sounds about right, sir."

"Well, there are applications on the table outside my office. I wish you luck."

"Thanks, man," Patch said. Dick gave him a parting wink.

As he headed away from Deep Springs and down to the road where he could hitch a ride to the airport, Patch felt, for maybe the first time ever, that there was one thing he really had to do. No choice about it. He was just a Deep Springs kind of guy.

That realization filled him with a need to locate his New York dudes immediately. After all, if he was going to end up here without them, he definitely needed to get back to them. And now.

Sarah Lawrence looked kind of like Vassar to me—vast lawns, old stately brick buildings—except somewhat more modest in scale. The buildings were more like something you would find on a private estate, because that's what it used to be. The entryway wasn't as dramatic either, just a tasteful wrought-iron structure. By eight o'clock on Friday evening, we hadn't made it much past that gate.

The traffic was brutal, and when we arrived on campus our limo was mobbed by Sarah Lawrence kids eager to catch a glimpse of Mickey. Apparently Mickey was an even bigger celebrity here than he was in Manhattan. There was word of various naked art events planned for tomorrow night, after the lecture. Also, we heard a rumor that the security staff was freaking out because they didn't know how they were going to keep the occupancy in the lecture hall from exceeding its maximum. That's how big the interest in Mickey Pardo was.

When I got out to take a piss there were at least fifteen people in the car, and a kind of impromptu party had started happening around it, too. Arno called that he was coming with me, and by the time we had fully extracted ourselves from the mob, there was no way to get back to tell Mickey and David we were taking off. "I don't think we're getting back in there," I said.

"That's better for me, anyway," Arno said as we looked around for a discreet tree. "Hey man, I hope you don't feel like I'm ditching you. But I think I'm going to take off and see if I can find Lara."

"Really?" I said, thinking about Gabby, who seemed kind of fun when I met her at the fundraiser. But who was I to judge? "That's cool man. I guess I can't really say anything, cuz I'm going to go find a girl, too."

"Yeah? That's cool."

I looked at the Tudor-style building we were coming up to and saw a bunch of kids sitting at café tables on the terrace, watching a black and white movie that was projected onto a wall. "I think that's where I'm going to find her, actually. She was telling me about this cinema club that meets on Friday nights, and how it's one of the reasons she wants to come here. She said it was really neat."

"Neat?"

"I know, but I think I really like her."

Arno tried to do his special handshake with me, but I couldn't remember how to do it, and in the end we just knocked fists. "See you later, man," he said, and walked off in the direction of the dorms.

I stepped onto the terrace and surveyed the scene. It was mostly girls, maybe one or two guys, and everybody was dressed pretty casually. Somehow, the whole tribe thing seemed much less in evidence here. I was wondering why that would be when I heard someone whisper my name.

"Jonathan, over here." I looked, and there was Ava, sitting on a folding chair. She was wearing a stretchy black pencil skirt and a vintage T-shirt. I went over and sat next to her on the ground. "This is my sister, Jill," she continued in a whisper. I shook hands with Jill, who was also sitting on the ground.

"Hi," I whispered. "What are we watching?"

"Actually," Jill said in a voice a little bit louder than the whisper the event called for, "this was all getting a little boring, and my co-op is having a party. We were only waiting around because Ava thought you might show up." I saw Ava elbow her sister when she said this. "So you want to come to the party or what?"

As we walked, Ava asked me about the trip up, and I tried to downplay the whole partying in the limo thing. I knew when we had gotten to Jill's co-op house, because Bessie Smith was playing and people were sitting on the porch smoking cigarettes. "It's like old-timey night or some shit," Jill said as we walked up the stairs. She gestured at the smokers. "I don't know who those people are."

It was warm in the kitchen, and people were sitting around a table playing cards. A few people looked up and gave us little waves, but mostly everyone remained fixated on the game. "Euchre," Jill said. "Have you ever played euchre?"

I shook my head.

"It's sort of like bridge. Old-lady game. And look what we have to drink! Hot buttered rum, *ultimate* old-lady drink. You kids want some?"

I wasn't sure I did, but I nodded anyway. Jill ladled out two cups for us from the big pot on the stove, and Ava and I sat down on stools in the corner of the room.

"Sorry about what happened with Lily," I said. "I hope you don't think I'm a freak."

"Yeah, that was weird," she said. "But *you're* not a freak."

"Phew," I said, knowing that my brother had already cleared things up with Lily using his magical Ted powers. Then, to change the subject, "This really seems like more of a winter drink."

Ava took a sip of her hot rum and nodded. "But you know, college kids and their concept nights. They don't conform to the calendar the rest of us use."

"Huh," I said. "So what do you think so far?"

Ava wrinkled her nose. "I don't know, college is weird. Seems like everyone is trying out a new pose, you know?"

"Yeah," I said. I took a deep breath. "But I kind of like that about college—it seems like a chance to change yourself into a newer, better person. You know what I mean?"

"No," Ava laughed. I was glad she finally laughed, because she had been acting kind of shy so far. "Why would I want to change myself?"

"Well, I don't think *you* need to change," I said. "But I used to be a really superficial person. New York kind of does that to you. And I think college might be my opportunity to not be like that anymore."

Ava laughed again, and put her hand on her chest in mock protest. "No guy who handles heirloom tomatoes with the care that you do could possibly be superficial."

For the first time all week, I felt a little burst of acceptance. If a do-gooder like Ava thought I was okay, I had to be, right?

We kept on talking like that for a long time, while the college kids played their granny game and the hot rum drink got drunk up. Later, when I felt like I was getting really good at getting Ava to laugh, Jill came back and told us it time for me to go.

"The thing is, we're planning a protest tomorrow," she said, putting her arms around her little sister. "It's hard always having to make the world a better place, but that's what we were brought up to do."

"Okay," I said, not wanting the warmth of the evening to end. "Maybe I can help? I want to make the world a better place."

Jill raised her eyebrows at me. "Sure. Just be here at noon, okay?"

I stood up awkwardly. Ava gave me one of those happy/groggy smiles, and I wished I could kiss her. But her sister didn't budge from where she was, so I just waved and told myself that I'd be seeing them tomorrow.

Arno knew she was there, instinctually. He had been walking the campus grounds a little aimlessly and then, all of a sudden, he caught a whiff of cigarette smoke and his heart went crazy.

There she was, sitting on the steps of one of the dormitories with her elbows rested delicately on her knees. "You're back," Lara said, exhaling.

"I've actually never been here."

"I meant back in a more figurative sense."

"Oh. Well, I would have been back sooner, but I knew I wanted to be mature enough for what happens between us. I think I'm ready now," he said. She looked at him blankly, so he added: "Also, I didn't know your last name."

She didn't move except to raise one long, dark eyebrow. It was such an Arnolike move it was almost creepy. "Lara Moreno. You've never heard of Moreno Wines?"

"Um . . ." Arno wished he had drunk more wine over the last week. *That* would have been grownup.

"Lara Sparkling White? It's delicious."

"I'll bet it is."

"My dad named it after me. Because I'm so bubbly." She rolled her eyes and stubbed out her cigarette. Then she stood up, brushed off the lap of her crew-neck white cashmere mini-dress, and walked toward Arno. She was wearing the same knee-high boots she had been wearing the night Arno saw her in his sleep, and her hair was in the same, slightly off ponytail. "Some grad student friends of mine are having a dinner party," she said huskily. "Do you want to come?"

And then she took his hand—because, of course, he wanted to—and they walked across campus to the little colony of old servants quarters that had been turned into grad-student housing.

"Lara!" exclaimed the woman who opened the door. "I was wondering when you'd show."

"Hey, Mel. This is my friend Arno, from the city," Lara said, after kissing both of Mel's cheeks. Mel took a step back and surveyed him. She was tall, with big hay-colored hair, and she was wearing a red sixties-style house dress with a cinched waist.

"Come on kids," she said, ushering them in.

The apartment was stacked with books and papers, and there were a bunch of pale people sitting around a large, utilitarian table and making a lot of noise.

"*That's* not what Derrida said," a guy with wire-frame glasses and a brush of reddish hair said as he reached past the bowls of pasta and salad to cut himself a corner of cheese. The ceilings were low, and the room was lit by candles. Arno noticed several rustic cracks in the walls.

"Pull up a chair, whichever chair you can find," Mel said as she sat in the lap of the Derrida guy. Then she poured big glasses of wine, which were passed down the table in Arno and Lara's direction. Everyone made welcome noises.

Arno didn't see any chairs, but he did locate a crate. He pulled it up to the table and then Lara sat down on his lap. As the Derrida guy justified his point, she listened and started idly playing with Arno's hair. He stopped listening to the Derrida argument entirely and focused instead on the musky smell of the girl in his lap.

"So what do you study?" asked an elfin girl sitting next to him. She was wearing a lot of eye-shadow and smoking.

"I don't," Arno said. "I live in the city."

"His parents are art dealers," Lara said.

"Oh yeah?"

"Wildenburger Gallery," Arno said proudly. It sounded very grown-up.

The elfin girl whistled. "Not bad. You going into the business?"

Arno shrugged. "The art interests me, but not the dealing." He thought that was a pretty good reply.

"Valerie is in art history," Lara explained. "She's brilliant."

"Mmm," Valerie said. "Well, maybe you're an academic then? We live in a more rarefied world, you see. Nothing ever gets bought or sold in academia."

Arno nodded. He took a grown-up sip of wine and congratulated himself on arriving here, in this very mature world of big ideas. And he fit in, he felt sure. How many guys his age had been in love twice in one week? He was the kind of dark-eyed romantic misfit who just falls in love easily . . .

All the gaunt faces around the dinner table were saying brash, interesting things, and Arno knew that he was where he was supposed to be. And he was relieved that he'd done all that hard work over the past week—which had caused him to miss *both* of his therapy sessions—to ensure a mature relationship with the gorgeous woman on his lap.

Mickey stumbled up the back stairs of one of the big, modern dormitories, behind a girl wearing a miniskirt and messy hair. He'd left David in the limo with all the other girls who had been hitting on him before he took off with this girl to see the stars from the roof of her dorm. This seemed mildly unjust to Mickey. But before he could continue this train of thought, he realized he was winded and had to pause.

"Tori," he called, "wait up."

"We're almost there, Mickey. Hurry up," she said in her adorable, slightly chipmunky voice.

He saw her silhouette in the doorway that led onto the roof, and chugged up the rest of the stairs. Then Tori grabbed his hand and they walked out onto the roof where the sky was already turning purple.

"Isn't it beautiful?" she sighed.

"Yeah, totally," Mickey said. He came up behind her and put his arms around her waist. She twisted around, staring up at him, and slipped her hand under Mickey's terry-cloth robe so that it rested against his chest. For a minute this annoyed him—she wasn't Philippa, what did she think she was doing?—but then he realized that was stupid. He was going to have to try dating again at some point. So he blew against her neck, which caused her to burst into weird giggles.

"That limo's pretty impressive," she said when she managed to stop laughing. They could see the limo below, and all the people who were leaning up against it.

"You seen one limo . . ." Mickey broke off in order to nibble on Tori's neck again.

"You must have done something pretty special to deserve a limo like that."

"You haven't heard about my lecture on nudity in public places in contemporary art?"

"Yeah," Tori said, giggling for no discernable reason. Mickey reminded himself not to compare her to Philippa. "I heard about it."

"Yeah? Because I'm doing something even bigger and bolder this time around."

"Really? Does anybody know?"

"Nope," Mickey said, lifting her chin with the knuckle of his index finger. "Just you."

Tori smiled and giggled again. She had recently applied red lipstick, but she didn't seem to have done her best work. At the moment it struck Mickey as poignant.

"Do you want to see them?"

"Okay."

Mickey pulled a small white box of slides from the pocket of his bathrobe, and led her, tottering a little bit, over to the fluorescent light by the doorway to the stairs. He removed one slide—of a classic SoHo street, empty at dawn—and held it up to the light. She narrowed her eyes at the image.

"Okay," she said.

"Just wait," Mickey said. But he didn't want to wait. He pulled out the picture he was most proud of, which showed him approaching the camera naked from the end of a subway car. The slight shaking of the car gave it a ghostly quality that Mickey especially liked.

"What do you think?"

Tori squinted. "Is that you?"

"Yup."

Tori gasped, and then she slapped him. It was a good hard slap, and Mickey was stunned for a moment. By the time he collected himself, Tori was all the way at the bottom of the first flight of stairs—he could tell from the clicking of her heels.

He rubbed his sore check and wondered at the powerful effect of his art. Surely that explained the slap, just like in that famous story in which Marcel Duchamp first exhibited his Mona Lisa with mustache and some foxy Parisienne slapped him across the face. If Mickey was remembering the story correctly, it ended with the Parisienne telling Duchamp he was a genius.

Mickey looked over the railing and saw Tori running into the Sarah Lawrence night. He rubbed his check and reminded himself that it was better to be free. And, possibly, a genius.

it's not breakfast at tiffany's, but i'll take it

When I woke up in the Sarah Lawrence admissions office, I felt surprisingly refreshed, and that was even before I discovered the coffee and donuts that had been set up in their little waiting area. I slipped into the bathroom and used water to sort of get my hair in place and make myself a little more protest-ready. Then I peaked into the office of Jenny Markal, the nice woman who let me in late last night.

"You sleep okay?" she asked me. She was wearing a headband and twin set.

"Yeah. And thanks for letting me in, by the way. Did you get your work done?" When I had come by last night, still a little queasy from the hot buttered rum and unable to locate my guys, she had been going over the students who would be attending in the fall and trying to figure out whom to accept off the waitlist. She made a little growling frustration noise now. "Go have fun, and try not to think about applications for as long as you can manage. And when you do, try and keep your essay to 500 words, okay?''

I said I would try. Then I waved, donut in mouth, and made my way out onto the campus, which was just as leafy and full of Frisbees and open notebooks as you might imagine.

When I got to Jill's co-op house, I saw that it looked a lot different by day—more airy and open. There were people lounging on the porch swing and on the front steps, which added to the general wholesomeness. Not ironic wholesome, but actually wholesome, with its white cornices and modest cherry trees out front. Also, there was a group of girls bending over an art project that they seemed to be working on ardently. Ava jumped up from this group.

''Jonathan, where have you been?'' she said. She was wearing navy gauchos and a white U-neck that revealed all the freckles splattered across her collar bones, and her hair was back in an effortless ponytail.

''Admissions office,'' I said, offering her the other half of my donut.

''Really?'' she asked, taking a thoughtful bite.

''It was all breakfast, no schmooze.''

"Come on, we're making masks," she said, taking my hand and dragging me onto the porch. Her palm had that magical thing so rare in palms—it was warm without being damp.

"For what?"

"For the protest, of course."

Jill gestured hello but didn't say anything because she was holding a paintbrush between her teeth. Then she handed me one of the many papier-mâché masks that were scattered around on the floor. I smiled at the other girls, who smiled but kept on at what they were doing.

"Why do we need masks?" I asked.

"Well," Jill said, "we don't *need* them of course. But it's sort of in the spirit of masked protest, you know what I mean? Like the Zapatistas or the Guerrilla Girls."

"Oh, right," I said. Were those names supposed to mean something to me? I made a mental note to Google them later.

"We're doing animals, see?" Ava said. "Look, I made you a penguin!"

Ava handed me the penguin mask, and I had to admit, with its widow's peak and yellow nose, it was pretty adorable. "Thanks," I said, hoping she didn't ask me anything else about penguins.

"Aw, that's sweet. But we gotta get going. The lecture's in like an hour and the paint still has to dry."

I looked up at Jill to see if she was kidding. Maybe about the sweet part, but there was no reason to believe the word "lecture" had been uttered in jest. "Lecture?" I said meekly. "What lecture?"

"The lecture we're protesting, of course."

"Which is . . . ?" I felt like a miniature bomb was about to go off in my throat.

Jill sighed heavily. "Every other Saturday they have a visiting artist speak—nearly always male, and the guy they have this week is a real creep. Just a showman, really. He took all these pictures of naked girls in a restaurant, and he projects them real big on a screen. Well, we call that sexism around here. And we're protesting it."

"Mickey's not a creep," I said. A girl with thin, set lips, who had been busy making a bear mask, looked up at me sharply. You could just tell that she wore her hair the same boring way every day.

"You know him?"

"Yeah, he's a friend of mine. I can't protest my friends." I looked at Ava, whose cheeks were turning pink, which made her eyes look especially crystalline. She looked at me and then quickly back at Jill. They did some eye-talking, and then Jill sighed.

"Look, Jonathan, you're not a creep, and I'm sure your friend Mickey isn't, either. But this whole campus has lost its head and we want to make a statement against the absurdity."

"That's just not a thing I would do to a friend," I said. I looked at Ava, and wondered if she was wondering if I were a really bad person. Or if she already knew it.

Some of the other girls who were involved in the mask-making were listening in now, too. "It's not even really about your friend," Ava said.

"That's true, actually," Jill said. "The thing that we want to make a statement about has nothing to do with your friend per se. It has to do with the fact that a disproportionate amount of money goes to male artists—and male art historians, and male lecturers—while at the same time, a lot of the art they're selling and writing and talking about prominently features T & A."

"Which, you have to admit, is a dynamic at work here," the girl with the thin lips said.

I nodded. "So you're not going to heckle him or anything?"

"Heckling was not on the agenda," Jill confirmed.

"Jill and I have been to about a million protests, and they're always fun," Ava added brightly.

"I do think the art world is a pretty ridiculous place," I said hesitantly. "A lot of my friends' parents are in that business, and it's not very kind to women."

"Hell, it doesn't even pay them," said the girl with the thin lips. "Except to take their shirts off."

"I've always thought there should be equal opportunities for women," I could hear my voice getting louder. If I was going to care, I should care about this, right? "I mean, I'd do anything for that."

Ava seemed to be making an I-told-you-so face at her sister. "I think that's beautiful," Jill said. "Now get working, because, like I said, the Mickey Pardo protest is in less than two hours."

When he woke up, Arno's head was foggy and the bed he was in was once again not his own. He sat up and blinked his eyes, and then lay back down. On the pillow next to his was a pile of sleek, dark hair. He was exactly where he'd wanted to be all week.

"Lara . . . ," he whispered.

The twin bed they'd slept on was so small that they were forced to spoon—not that Arno minded—and he could feel her lank, warm body next to his. For a moment, Arno glimpsed the future: small, spare rooms, lofty ideas, and Lara next to him through it all. His vision practically dripped with meaning.

"Lara . . . ," he whispered again.

She jerked around in the bed, and then pulled up her eye mask to look up at him. If he hadn't known better, he'd have thought the look on her face was surprise.

"Oh, hello," she said flatly, and then rolled out of the bed, taking the sheet with her. She stumbled across the floor, took a cigarette from the top of the dresser and lit it. She moved to the twin bed opposite the one they'd slept in and sat down in her sheet toga. She stared at Arno while twisting her hair in a knot on the top of her head.

Lara didn't look as lovely as she had last night—her skin was blotchy, and the scowl wasn't very flattering either—but Arno reminded himself that this was a meaningful relationship. In a meaningful relationship, looking good wasn't *always* important; you were bound to see your lover when she was not at her most gorgeous and you just got over it.

"Arno," she said, "what are you still doing here?"

"What?" Arno felt like he was in some sub-reality. "We slept together last night."

"Yeah, I know," Lara said. "But that doesn't really answer my question, does it? What are you still *doing* here?"

"Well, I mean, I slept here, and now I'm awake so . . ."

"Let me rephrase the question. Why haven't you *left* yet?"

Arno wished his mind was moving quicker, because he was having trouble comprehending Lara's words and tone. He closed his eyes for a moment, and then started over. "Well, in a meaningful relationship you wake up beside the other person, right?"

"What meaningful relationship?" Lara asked, taking a drag of her cigarette.

"Um . . . *ours*?" he replied. When Lara raised an irritated eyebrow, he continued, "I did it—I was in love with someone else. First love, naïveté, I've done all that. Now I'm ready to be in love with *you* and have a meaningful relationship and everything that goes along with it."

Lara made a scoffing noise. "Listen, I got over relationships way back in the fall of my freshman year."

"What?" Arno knew his bottom lip was hanging down like a baby's, but he couldn't help it.

Lara sighed impatiently and took a last drag of her cigarette before flicking it in the direction of the window. "Arno, I was just using you for sex, you get it? Now would you clear out of here? I have a lot of studying to do today."

Arno's heart was somewhere down near his feet now. He didn't understand how a girl who was so complex and mysterious could behave the same way superficial New York party girls did. How could studying be more important than this relationship that he'd been working toward all week? But he did understand that he had to leave the room. Now. To be followed shortly, he hoped, by the dorm itself. And then Sarah Lawrence altogether.

"I am so glad you're here," Lourdes Soto, the chair of the Sarah Lawrence Art Department said, as she ushered Mickey into the small room adjacent to the lecture hall. She appeared to be out of breath. "The crowd is getting restless."

"This is my friend David," Mickey said. He looked rumpled and smelled slightly of beer and he knew it, but he had at least succumbed to David's pleas and put on a pair of pin-striped pants and a white T-shirt instead of the white terry-cloth robe he had been sporting for the previous twenty-four hours. "He's also my assistant. Can you arrange to have a chair for him onstage?"

"Yes, of course," Professor Soto said. She had dark auburn hair collected in a bun at the nape of her neck, and, in her neat black suit, she looked much more grown up and academiclike than Mickey remembered her being.

She stepped aside and spoke to a graduate student who had just come in. The graduate student then disappeared, apparently to fetch the chair. "I have some bad news," Professor Soto said as she returned to them. "They had to tow the limo. But don't worry. We'll have the vehicle back by the end of the lecture so that you can have it for your personal use for the rest of the week-end."

Mickey glared at Professor Soto and then said, "That's fine, Lourdes. Can you have these put in a slide carousel for me? They're in order." He could feel David shifting nervously behind him, and he nudged him to toughen up.

"Of course," Professor Soto said. Another grad student appeared with a slide carousel, and when he had finished arranging the slides Professor Soto told him to set them up in the lecture hall. "Shall we?" she asked, extending her arm to Mickey.

Mickey let her lead him onto the stage. A hush fell over the audience as David and then Mickey took their seats. Mickey could tell by the way girls were craning their necks that they were trying to figure out if it was the David from the pictures, and he leaned over to tell David so in a loud whisper. Then they both listened as Professor Soto praised Mickey as well as the college for being able to woo the most provocative minds of the coming generation for their Saturday-afternoon lecture series.

After her remarks there was light applause, and then Mickey approached the lectern.

"Well," Mickey began with a chortle, "you already know who I am. Professor Soto was just very kind in her opening remarks, and, of course, unless you've been living under a rock for the last week"—the audience roared—"you've heard of my work exploring nudity in public places."

Mickey grinned at his fans, who had packed into every corner of the room like little toy soldiers. They were all eager to see what he had to show them. He also noted with satisfaction that a student wearing a red-and-white vest that said fire marshall on it was walking up and down the aisles anxiously clearing a path in case of an emergency.

"But tonight I have something new for you. Think of it as a journey. Lights please." The lights dimmed, and Mickey clicked to his first slide. It projected a skyline of New York, with setbacks and rooftop gardens and water towers lit from behind by the early morning light. It was the view from the roof of the Pardo townhouse.

Mickey seemed to remember a lot of effortless and hilarious banter the last time he'd lectured, but he was really tired at the moment, so he decided to go for a more hands-off approach. Maybe it would be mysterious? He clicked through the pictures of architectural façades and cityscapes, which he had carefully arranged so they moved downward. Into the depths of the city— that's what he'd told himself. Occasionally, he punctuated a picture with a few words: "urban decay," or "hazy morning," or "bodega."

The audience was so quiet he wondered if he'd put a spell on them. Then he heard someone call, "Where's the skin?" He looked over to Professor Soto, who was looking apprehensively at the audience, and then he went on.

Mickey clicked forward to the first picture that included himself. "Flesh," he said.

On the screen behind him, an image of a cobblestone street appeared. There was a wall of plastered advertisements on one side of the picture, and on the other was Mickey Pardo's naked behind as he dashed out of the picture frame. The audience made a noise that wasn't exactly awe.

Mickey flicked through several similar pictures.

"What interests me here," he said, "is the contrast between bodies and buildings, bone and steel."

There was a loud cough from the audience. Mickey was acutely aware of someone getting up and leaving. He flicked to a picture of himself lying on top of his terry-cloth robe under the Washington Square arch. "There is a beauty in what's fallen," he said.

"Oh, come *on*," someone from the audience said.

Mickey ignored this, and clicked to a picture of him standing proudly on top of a trash can. "But the city always rises above."

"Who are you and what have you done with Mickey Pardo?" cried a girl sitting close to the back. There was snickering throughout the lecture hall.

"This is boring!" someone else called.

Mickey clicked his slide emphatically. "Is there a problem?" he said into the microphone. Feedback screeched in his ears. There was some loud grumbling, and for a minute it appeared that nobody was going to be brave enough to say anything.

"We want ass!" a voice near the front of the lecture hall cried. More grumbling followed, mixed with applause.

Mickey turned toward David with a desperate look.

"Keep going," David whispered. "It's just a rocky start."

Mickey looked back at the audience. "The city, like the body, never shuts down . . . ," he said into the microphone.

"Is this cheap philosophizing what my parents paid forty thousand dollars for?" Someone else called. "Cuz it's definitely not worth that much!"

"Ass, ass, ass!" A group of girls in the mezzanine were chanting.

"Yeah, we came for ass, not a full frontal shot of your serious little willy!" Mickey wasn't even sure where the voices were coming from anymore. He was getting damp under the armpits, and he could smell beer on himself, which only reminded him that he would rather be drinking a nice cold beer right now instead of lecturing to people who didn't get him.

A guy in a worn T-shirt and black jeans stood up, somewhere in the middle of the lecture hall. "This is bull," he started in a high whiny tone. "This is a total vanity photo project that we've all been duped into wasting our Saturday afternoon on. Not to mention that it is total crap that the college can spend thousands of dollars to get this guy to come talk, but they can't even provide studios for all the senior art majors."

Suddenly, everyone was yelling. Mickey rolled his eyes and turned to Professor Soto for assistance. He looked just in time to see her dashing into the adjacent room. David jumped up to bring her back, but he found the door locked, and he turned to give Mickey a frightened shrug.

"I mean really," a girl in the front row called up to him, "were you ever cool, or was it all just hype?"

"It's not hype," Mickey said desperately. "I'm the real deal!"

This seemed to make it worse. Everyone was yelling

now, and the whole back row was chanting, "Go home! Go home! Go home!"

Mickey turned his bloodshot eyes on David.

"I don't understand," Mickey said.

"Me neither," David said. His eyes were also bloodshot, but the sight of him was comforting to Mickey nonetheless.

"We gotta get out of here," Mickey said.

"Let's go."

"No—not yet. I can't leave it like this. There might be a riot. You go—round up the guys. I'll pacify 'em, and meet you outside in fifteen."

David gave Mickey a long, hard look. "Are you sure?"

"Just go!"

"Does a girl have to be *naked* to get *lectured* about on *campus*?" Jill yelled at some of the stragglers who were still cramming their way into Sarah Lawrence's main lecture hall. They looked at her, confused, and we all jostled our signs in their direction and clapped rhythmically five times. There were about seven girls and me, standing on the walk to the lecture hall, on a bright, cloudless, and very collegiate day.

"Celebrate—don't exploit—women artists! Woohoo!"

Two boys and a girl walking to the lecture hall still looked confused. They gave us thumbs-ups and disappeared inside. We had already watched what seemed like every person on campus go into the lecture hall, and now we were just sitting outside chanting to ourselves, mostly.

"This is way more fun than I thought it would be," I said. And I didn't even have to try to say it. I really meant it. Being outside and making a big fuss about all the bad out there felt really frickin' good.

"I know, isn't it neat?" Ava laughed. She was wearing the tiger mask I'd made for her, and I was still wearing my penguin one. "Jill and I come from this really political family. Some families go to Hawaii together—*we* had to march on Washington." She rolled her eyes like it was ridiculous, but I could tell that this was how she thought of herself.

"Do you think we had any effect?" I asked Jill.

"Absolutely. I mean, we go to school with a bunch of sheep anyway. But trust me. The subversive message is lodged in their brains now." She cackled faux-maniacally.

Another group of stragglers went by, and we jostled our signs again and made a variety of animal noises. Because I had no idea what kind of noises penguins made, I went for the rooster noise. This group was wearing those oversized T-shirts with naked people on the front, which struck me as really sophomoric. They peered at us, trying to figure out who was behind the masks.

"Equal pay for equal work!" the girls chanted.

"Save the penguins!" I added.

"Hell no, we won't go!" one of the girls in our group yelled. The kids walked on. We all clapped for each other.

I was starting to realize that one of the coolest parts of caring about something and making it known is how it catches everyone off guard. They all just stare at you with these funny expressions on their faces. It's sort of like riding around town in a Mini Cooper.

It was right around the time that we start chanting about all the inequities of the world, and not just women in the arts, that I noticed a strange trend. There were still some people going into the lecture hall, but now people were starting to leave it, too. The people who were leaving didn't bother looking at us. They look pissed and all riled up.

"Maybe our message has taken effect already?" the thin-lipped girl said. (I had since discovered that her name was Sylvia and that she was the president of the campus chapter of the National Organization for Women, which explained the big, purple NOW shirt that was currently dwarfing her small frame.)

"Doubtful," Jill said. "Maybe once was enough for your buddy Mickey?"

I felt a twinge of disloyalty, but then Ava gave

me an apologetic look, and I remembered that what I was doing out here had more to do with the thousands of years of patriarchal domination than it did with one measly little art presentation.

But I knew that wasn't entirely valid.

Then, just to turn the scene really bizarre, a guy in overalls went running by us, yelling, "We want ass! We want ass!"

I knew something was wrong now, and the guilt was intensifying—that's when I saw my friend David come running out of the lecture hall. I smiled, because the sight of David made me childishly happy for a moment. But then my smile faded, because one look at him told me that something was very, very wrong.

Arno felt his body go limp, and then he just let it sort of fall into the big, forgiving oak tree that he had been hiding behind. Since he'd flipped off the former love of his life and dashed from her room, he'd been slinking around campus trying to get back to his friends without being seen by the Cruelest Woman in the World—i.e., Lara.

Actually he was afraid that if she saw him, and he saw her, that he would just burst into tears. Although secretly he really *did* want to run into her. Then she would see him cry, and she would know that he was more than just a face. That he was also a big jumble of feelings and ideas, and that he hurt.

He placed his hand on his chest, near his heart. It felt like a big, soggy, tear-soaked mass, but it was still beating. He knew it was still beating.

He dashed to the next tree. Across the lawn he spotted the lecture hall—all he had to do was get himself there.

But then he felt his phone vibrate in his pocket, reminding him that he had a message. He pulled it out and clicked through his new text messages.

The were all from Gabby. In order, they read:

cant decide what to wear call me
where are u? going to party alone
at party where are u?
where are u?
going home

Arno's heart felt soggy and heavy all over again. He didn't understand how he could have moronically followed this conniving, evil girl to her evil campus lair when someone sweet and fun was waiting for him in her Lower East Side, parent-free, studio apartment.

There was only one thing to be done. He dialed Gabby's number and listened with great anticipation to the one ring before it went to voicemail.

Hey, this is Gabby's phone. Heart you!

Arno sighed heavily. "Gabby, this is Arno. I am a very flawed guy as you've probably discovered. I thought I was in love with somebody else, but it was a lie. I was using you so that I could fall in love with her, but really you were the one I was in love with all along. What I've done is unforgivable, but maybe you could find it in your heart to do that, and, you know, forgive me. Gabby, please give me a second chance."

Arno hung up, feeling that his heart was lighter already. He made a dash for the lecture hall.

david *still* can't help it if he looked great naked

David tried to slip as inconspicuously as possible down the aisle as the shouts of protest rose against his friend. But, of course, he was still six-five, and the image of him in the buff was still ingrained in the minds of many of the audience members. They reached out and grasped at his hands as he passed.

When he emerged into the bright and green outdoors, he had to close his eyes to adjust to the light. When he opened them, he saw that he was surrounded by people in animal masks.

A short person in a bear mask and big purple shirt was moving toward him. "It's him," she said sharply, "the guy from the photographs. He's one of the cronies of the patriarchy."

Two other animal-faced people stepped up behind the bear. "Crony of the patriarchy! Crony of the patriarchy!" they chanted.

David couldn't believe this was happening, and he was trying not to freak out. He opened his mouth to protest, and then another person—this one in a crow mask—joined in. "Did you know that women still make seventy-five cents for every dollar a man makes?"

"Um, no. But I don't really make any money, so . . ."

"The position you hold in the patriarchy makes you complicit," the crow snapped.

"Did you know that in this country a woman is sexually assaulted every two and a half minutes?" the bear added.

"I mean, that's awful," David stammered.

The people in animal masks—David had now figured out that they were girls—stepped toward him. "Awful doesn't begin to describe it."

Just as David was wondering whether he shouldn't take his chances with the angry art fans, instead of the angry feminists, two more people joined the group. David knew instantly that the one in the penguin mask was a dude. Then he took the mask off.

David felt shock and anger and relief all at once.

"This is my friend David," Jonathan said to the animal-faced crowd. "He's one of the good guys."

"Sorry, Jonathan," one of the masked girls said, "it's really nice that you're down with the cause and everything, but this guy was pictured front and center in the restaurant photos. He's so patriarchal he doesn't even realize it."

Jonathan looked pained but adamant as he said, "Can't you hear yourself? He was pictured *front* and *center*. He was just as naked as all of the girls. It was a totally mixed group. And it was fun. Girls were having fun and guys were having fun. I mean *women*, the *women* were having fun."

Jonathan sighed and fidgeted with his penguin mask. Then he turned to a girl in a tiger mask. "I'm sorry, Ava," he said. "I think your cause is right on. I want you to have the same opportunities as I do, and I want to do everything in my power to make that possible. But I can't get with what you guys are saying about David. He's a super good guy, and he loves women. If there's no room in your activism for guys like us, who want equality for women, then I think that's just not right."

There was a long pause, and several of the masked feminists shifted on their feet. Then they started clapping. "You go, boy," one of them said.

Then Ava, the tiger girl, pushed up her mask. David was surprised—although he knew he shouldn't have been—to see that she was really pretty, with earthy freckles and clear blue eyes and shiny brown bangs brushed sideways across her face. She trembled a little bit and then she stepped forward and kissed Jonathan. David wished he had someone besides the bear girl to confirm what he was witnessing. But there it was, still happening—Jonathan and this tiger girl were very publicly making out.

"Psst . . ." David turned and saw Arno's head peaking around a tree. He tilted his head toward Jonathan and then Arno came hesitantly over. "What's going on?"

"No clue," David whispered. "Did you find that Lara girl?"

"She broke my heart."

"Oh. Bummer."

"Yeah, totally. Hey, can we get out of here?"

"Um, I think Jonathan is busy."

Just then, the doors to the lecture hall were flung open with a loud bang. David and Arno looked up and saw Mickey running in their direction with a mob of angry people behind him.

i know when it's time to go

When Ava kissed me I knew that I was on the right path to being a good person. My insides roared with good feelings, and I knew that in some crazy cosmic way I was being rewarded for trying so hard to find a cause to believe in. So I wasn't surprised that the whole world seemed to be roaring, too.

I felt Ava's lips part from mine, and then I looked up to see all the people we had just watched enter the lecture hall start to pour out. They were roaring, but not for me. Ahead of them, but not by much, was Mickey Pardo, and he looked deeply freaked out.

"What's going on?" I hissed at David.

"It all went to shit," he said. "I think we should really get out of here."

I noticed that Arno was right behind him, but I couldn't figure out what was going on. I looked back at Ava, who was still holding my hand. "You should go," she said regretfully. Then she pecked me on the mouth, and it was the softest, sexiest peck I'd every experienced. "But if you don't call me when you get back to the city, I'm going to picket your life."

I stared into her eyes for one last second, and then I turned to my guys. "Let's go!"

Mickey was right up behind us by then. "We gotta blow!" he was shouting. "Now!"

The crowd was growing now, and they were chanting, "Give our money back! Give our money back!"

So we ran. We ran for that tasteful wrought-iron gate we'd entered not twenty-four hours before, and as soon as we cleared it, we used all the strength we had to heave the thing shut. The art students were reaching the gates now, and they seemed really intent on taking something from us.

"They're definitely going to get through that thing," I said. As soon as the words were out of my mouth, a canary-yellow Mercedes came screeching toward us off the road.

"Patch!" we all shouted, out of surprise as much as joy. He stepped out of the car and gave us a lazy smile. He looked even more tanned and handsome than usual. The art crowd behind us was still yelling about their money, and happy as I was to see Patch, I really wanted to get my friends far away from Sarah Lawrence, and fast.

"Let's do it," I said, and we all went piling into the car.

Patch sat back into the driver seat. "Hey dudes," he said. Then he punched Mickey—who was in the front passenger seat—in the arm. "I'm really sorry I missed your art thing again, Bro."

"Forget it," Mickey said, looking wildy behind us. "Could you just step on it, please?"

Patch put the car into gear, and then we zipped onto the road, leaving all those bitter Sarah Lawrence art types behind.

"No man, I mean, I'm really sorry. I just . . . I had to get out for a while, go someplace, you know what I mean?"

"What happened?" I asked. Patch met my eyes in the rearview mirror.

"Greta made out with this ex-boyfriend of hers. She said it was a one-time thing and she's sorry, and part of me wants to get over it, you know? But another part of me thinks this a sign that it's time to move on. Anyway, I heard about this crazy school in California called Deep Springs. So that's where I went, to check it out."

"Man, that sucks," I said. "Are you all messed up about Greta?"

Patch shrugged. "I mean, we're cool. She's gotta do what she's gotta do, and I gotta do what I gotta do. Going to Deep Springs really helped. I think . . . that might be my place."

"Oh yeah?"

"Yeah," Patch sighed heavily, "I know we all talked about going to school together next year and how awesome that would be. But I think what I have to do is go to this little school in California where no one knows who I am, or thinks they do. Will you guys still like me if I abandon you for a couple years?"

I sort of had to laugh at that. "Patch, you're *always* abandoning us, and we always like you anyway."

The other guys nodded their agreement.

"And it's probably a good thing you missed my lecture," Mickey muttered. He shook his head. "I can't believe it got that ugly. I mean, were my pictures *that* bad?"

"I thought they were good," David said supportively.

"I mean, everyone loved them the first time around," I chimed in.

"Uh, this *was* the first time around," David said.

"What?"

"I had to take new pictures because Philippa hasn't come out to her parents. They were new pictures. Just pictures of the city when it's empty. Oh, and me, too."

"Naked?" I said.

"Yeah, naked."

"Mickey, don't take this the wrong way. But next time you do something like this, would you consult with me, please?"

"Well, I tried, but you had a Greenpeace thing. It was like you didn't have time for me, and that's when things got *messed* up."

"I know. Forgive me," I said. "I'll never do it again."

We were on the parkway now, heading down toward the city, which sounded pretty much like the only place I wanted to be. There was a pause, and then Arno spoke up.

"I really feel your pain on the Greta thing. I just got my heart stepped on, too."

"I knew Lara was bad news, man. I'm sorry that had to happen," I said. "I'm sorry I didn't say anything."

"It probably did have to happen," he said. "The ironic thing is that I thought being with her would make me more deep, but I think it's the *not* being with her that's teaching me all these new things about human nature and shit. Anyway, I'm just worried that Gabby won't talk to me anymore. I called her, though. Maybe she'll give me another shot."

We were all quiet. It seemed doubtful, but I figured Arno had already had enough bad news for one day so I didn't say anything.

"Girls"—David said softly, but before he could finish the thought his phone went off. He made a face and answered it. "Hi, Mom," he said. "Really? That's great . . . I mean, it's great for her . . . No, I know you did what you had to do. It's cool, I'm still your kid . . . I'll see you soon, okay, Mom? Bye."

He threw the phone on the floor and shouted, "Yes!"

"What happened?" I asked, sensing I was missing one last piece of the puzzle.

"Oh, well, during the week that you dropped out of our lives, I started dating Sara-Beth Benny. You remember how *Mike's Princesses* worked? The dad's a stand-up comic by night, plumber by day, and . . ."

"I'm familiar with the show, David."

"Oh, yeah. Anyway, she moved into the apartment and my parents started treating her and it just got sort of weird, you know? I felt like she was more my sister than my girlfriend, and they wanted me to do all this weird stuff."

I didn't want to know what kind of stuff, so I just said, "But it sounds like it all worked out?"

"Yeah, my mom just called to say that Sara-Beth got a part in this indie film and she flew to L.A. this morning." He paused like he was imagining what might have been. "She plays some kind of addict, apparently."

"Man, that sucks. You gonna miss her?"

"Sure, but it's not like I can't see the bright side."

And then I sort of had to start laughing. "Man you guys all got in a lot of trouble. Why didn't anyone *tell* me any of this?"

"You were too busy shopping around for something to care about," Arno said. "Going to fundraisers and shit."

"I'm sorry," I said, "I'll never do it again."

And even though I knew there was probably a fundraiser or two in my future, part of what I was saying was true. Because even before I'd had this whole caring panic attack, I had already really cared about something—my friends, and the lives they were trying to live. And that was something I was going to care about for a long time.

Don't miss *Girls We Love*, the sixth Insiders book, coming soon!

They've loved, lost, and totally obsessed, and now the Insiders' girls are out for revenge . . . even if it means turning the Insiders into real boyfriends. Find out about:

Flan: The youngest *and* the ringleader. She's ready for Jonathan to care about her . . . exclusively!

Philippa: Mickey's messed things up so many times, but he *does* love her. Can she turn him into the boy of her dreams?

Liesel: Remember that girl from uptown who drove Arno crazy? She's ba-*aack*.

Sara-Beth Benny: She's a star, and she wants David to be one, too. But can David fake feelings?

And Patch's mystery girl: He doesn't even know her, but boy, does she know him . . .

Watch out! The Insiders may never look at each other—or girls—the same way again.

While you wait, catch up with the guys at www.insidersbook.com.